RICH $AVAGE 3

Lock Down Publications and Ca$h
Presents

RICH $AVAGE 3

A Novel by *Martell "Troublesome" Bolden*

Rich $avage 3

Lock Down Publications
Po Box 944
Stockbridge, Ga 30281

Visit our website @
www.lockdownpublications.com

Lock Down Publications
Like our page on Facebook: Lock Down Publications @
www.facebook.com/lockdownpublications.ldp
Cover design and layout by: **Dynasty Cover Me**
Book interior design by: **Shawn Walker**
Edited by: **Kiera Northington**

Stay Connected with Us!

Text **LOCKDOWN** to 22828 to stay up-to-date with new releases,
sneak peaks, contests and more…
Thank you.

Submission Guideline.

Submit the first three chapters of your completed manuscript to ldpsubmissions@gmail.com, subject line: Your book's title. The manuscript must be in a .doc file and sent as an attachment. Document should be in Times New Roman, double spaced and in size 12 font. Also, provide your synopsis and full contact information. If sending multiple submissions, they must each be in a separate email.

Have a story but no way to send it electronically? You can still submit to LDP/Ca$h Presents. Send in the first three chapters, written or typed, of your completed manuscript to:

LDP: Submissions Dept
Po Box 944
Stockbridge, Ga 30281

DO NOT send original manuscript. Must be a duplicate.

Provide your synopsis and a cover letter containing your full contact information.

Thanks for considering LDP and Ca$h Presents.

Chapter 1

After all of the shit I've seen and done in these streets, I'm fortunate to still be free and alive. With so much money stackin' up and so many murders pilin' up, I know I gotta be on the lookout for twelve and opps. I'ont wanna end up gettin' snatched up by the feds like Baller. So, my best bet is to be careful with who I deal with, in order to avoid bein' snitched on, which is exactly why I'm skeptical of Phat. And I'ont wanna end up gettin' killed by a rival like Gee, so it's best I be on point and stay strapped in order to avoid bein' caught lackin', which is exactly why I smoked Stone. Shit, I ain't tryin' to go out either one of those ways, Ace contemplated. He realized most of the real ones was either indicted or murdered.

Ace couldn't help but to think about all of the shit he had been going through. After losing his lil brotha to some gunfire, Ace went on a rampage to kill the niggas responsible. And when he finally got the chance to get even with Stone, he did just that. Also, during his retaliation, Ace had gunned down Star, who happened to be with Stone the night of the murder. After he had seen Cavalier Johnson, the first Black elected mayor of Milwaukee, speak out about the heartless double-murder on *FOX6 News*, Ace learned that Stone and Star's toddler daughter was in the vehicle, strapped into her car seat while the murders had taken place. Frankly, Ace didn't give a fuck about making their daughter an orphan.

Now that Ace had offed Stone, he and his gang didn't have as much beef. Therefore, they could put more of their focus on runnin' up some paper-cheese. Although Ace was always strapped for beef, because he knew the more money he come across, the more problems he was bound to see. Thus far, he and his niggas had gotten their money and weight up in a major way. And Ace wanted all of them to glaze in the streets. However, his under-standing was the savage life would more than likely end with prison or death, and he was willing to accept either fate without snitchin' or foldin'. So, Ace wouldn't stop living the rich savage lifestyle.

Ace did know there was more to life. He needed to stay free and alive in order to be there for his family. It was no secret his girl, Paris, and their son, Adonis, meant everything to him. Not to mention, he had his big sista, Mika, to be there for. And things with his mom, Gale, was just beginning to get better. Ace knew he had more to live for than just himself.

While Ace was seated on the park bench thinking, he watched his girl push their son on the swing. Today, Ace was spending time with his family. He understood Paris appreciated when he spent time with them far more than when he spent money on them. Because materialistic things only last for so long, but memories will last forever.

The park was filled with kids and their parents having fun in the sun with no care in the world, although Ace was careful to tote his .45 Glock. He knew just as bad as twelve wanted to bury him under jail, opps wanted to bury him under dirt. Therefore, he would rather be caught dead with his gun than without it. Because more than his own life, Ace cared to protect the lives of his family. Even though he also put his life on the line for money, whips and jewelry, he recognized his most prized possessions was his girl and son.

Paris approached the bench, then took a seat beside Ace, while Adonis ran along and played amongst some other kids. She couldn't help but notice Ace seemed to have something on his mind. For the past few days, Paris could read he was more tranquil than lately. If only she knew it was because Ace had gotten some vindication.

Paris rested her head on Ace's shoulder and interlocked her fingers in his, then asked, "Ace, what's on your mind?"

"A lot of shit. But most importantly, you and our son," Ace said. He pecked her forehead then looked out at his son. "It feels good to know I finally got y'all outta the hood."

"And I really do love our new house. It's a better place to raise a family than that apartment."

With everything that was going down in the streets, Ace had decided to move his girl and son someplace put up. He had Paris find them a family home in a suburbia neighborhood about an hour away from the inner city of Milwaukee. Ace didn't want twelve or opps to be able to locate where he and his family lay their heads. He wanted to do all he could to keep them out of harm's way.

"Even though we got outta the hood, I'll never forget where I'm from, 'cause that shit made me a rich savage," Ace told her.

"And I respect who you are, Ace. Although all that being savage-hearted shit haven't gotten you nowhere. I know you love your hood but fuck your hood. Now you need to do more with yourself and live good," Paris laid out.

"I hear you, Paris." As hard as it was to do, Ace had to admit she had a valid point. Majority of the niggas from his hood had gotten locked up for drugs and murder or killed over petty beef. But that shit wouldn't prevent him from going back to the hood. Paris shifted towards him. "So, I been looking for a place to open the boutique, and I found one."

"Just figure out how much it costs to rent to own, then let me know."

"Alright. Bae, I appreciate you doing everything to help me with opening my own business."

"I just want for my girl to be on her shit, feel me? And I'ma buy you a new car too, 'cause I can't have my girl out here in that lil Honda Accord."

"For real, bae?"

"Yeah, I got you. Matter fact, go online right now and find you somethin' nice," he instructed her.

"Okay." Paris grabbed her iPhone out of her Birkin handbag, then went online to Carvana in search of some vehicles.

Ace saw Adonis tumble to the ground and start crying, so he went to make sure his son was okay. After checking on Adonis's wellbeing, Ace said, "Stop cryin', lil nigga, you okay. I ain't raisin' no punk."

"Me not a punk, Daddy," Adonis assured in his toughest tone. Ace chuckled as he dusted off his son's clothes. "I know you ain't. Now, go finish playin'." He returned to the bench as Adonis ran along.

"Look, bae, I like this car right here," Paris said and handed him the phone to see. She found herself a silver Porsche Macan T SUV, which was new, but used.

"That one's good." Ace handed her back the phone. "Go ahead and buy it."

"Okay." Paris did as instructed. She scheduled for the vehicle to be dropped off sometime tomorrow. "It's done. The car will be delivered to our house."

"That's cool with me," Ace said. "How 'bout we go and grab somethin' to eat?"

Paris called for Adonis, who came running towards his parents, and Ace scooped up his son into his arms. As they started towards Paris's Accord, Ace planted Adonis on the ground then raced him to the car. Paris placed Adonis into his car seat in the backseat, then she slid behind the wheel while Ace entered the passenger side. Once the family was all loaded into the car, they were off to their next destination.

Soon thereafter, they arrived at IHOP where Paris pulled into the parking lot and found a spot to park the Accord. Ace along with Paris and Adonis exited the car and then walked into the flapjack joint. After placing their orders, it wasn't long before the food was delivered to their table.

While Ace enjoyed his red velvet pancakes, Paris grabbed a napkin and wiped whipped cream from the corners of his mouth. "Boy, stop making such a mess of yourself." She used the same napkin to wipe Adonis's mouth too. "Both of y'all are messy eaters."

"Good lookin'," Ace replied. He peeped Paris studying him from across the table. "What?"

"I just get the feeling there's something more on your mind that you're not telling me."

"And what makes you think that?" He sipped at his drink.

"Because I know you," she answered, pointing her fork at him. "Is it your brother? Because I know you're still grieving over him."

Ace leaned back in his seat and let out a deep breath. "Well, somethin' like that." Part of him wanted to tell her about his getting revenge for Gee, but he felt the less she knew, the better. Instead, he said, "Ever since Gee got killed, I've been gettin' close to my ma. She'll be comin' home in a few months, and I wanna be there for her."

"Well, I can't wait to finally get the chance to meet her. I know you've had a strained relationship with her over the years, but it's good to see you really care about her. Plus, I think it'll be good for your mom and son to bond."

"Me too. And bein' that my ma didn't have a real bond with me, I want her to at least have one with Adonis, and any other kids we may have," Ace expressed.

Paris dropped her gaze down to her plate and she forked at her chocolate chip pancakes. "Ace, I'm sure your mother wants to bond with your son. But don't you think she need to bond with you also?" She returned her gaze to his. "She already lost your little brother to the streets, so I know it'll devastate her to lose you. It'll devastate me and your son, too."

"Paris, my ma knows how shit goes in these streets. Besides, y'all don't have to worry about losin' me no time soon."

"Keep living the way that you do then, sooner or later, you'll end up dead or prison, Ace." Paris's eyes were filled with emotion.

Ace peered straight into her eyes, and said, "Listen, believe me or not, my life and freedom means a lot to me. But I ain't gonna live in fear. Just know I'ma do my all to be here for y'all."

"I hope so," Paris replied. "Now, let's finish our meals."

Looking across the table at his girl and son, Ace saw just how innocent they were and couldn't stomach the thought of putting them in harm's way due to his life as a savage. Just because he was a certified street nigga that didn't mean he wasn't also a family man. However, Ace had to do his all to stay free and alive in order to take care of his family. And he understood what makes people family is loyalty, so he couldn't put his trust into many.

Because oftentimes greed, envy, and jealousy will breed betrayal from those close. Therefore, Ace mainly trusted his pistol and slugs, and he would murk anyone that became a threat to his family, freedom, and life.

Chapter 2

"Look, just gimme about an hour and I'll be there," Ace told his clientele before ending the call. He was lying in bed at Savvy's crib when he had been awakened by his trap-phone ringing. It was a call about a play for four and a half ounces of hard crack.

Glancing at the time on the phone's display, Ace saw it was close to ten in the morning. He noticed there were some missed calls and unread text messages, but he didn't bother to answer. There was money to be made and no time to waste.

Ace's side-bitch remained sound asleep as he sat up on edge of the bed then stretched and yawned. He rose to his feet in only his boxer-briefs and walked into the adjacent bathroom, where he took a piss. After pissing, Ace returned to the bedroom and went to the stash spot, which was in the closet beneath the floorboards. All of his guns, drugs, and cash was there, along with some of Savvy's possessions. He grabbed out two ounces of soft coke and then took it into the kitchen where he would whip up the work.

When he had first started trappin' at the age of thirteen, Ace had been taught the whip game by Baller. Once Ace gathered the utensils and ingredients he would use for the cook up, then he turned on the stove to four hundred degrees, poured water into the glass coffee pot, and placed it onto the fired up stove top. As the water boiled, he added both ounces of cocaine and added the right amount of baking soda by eyeball measurement. This way he could stretch the dope and still have it come back as straight-drop, instead of baking soda residue. Next, with a flick of the wrist, he whipped the mixture of powdered substances, using a straightened-out iron clothes hanger, and fumes of the cooking crack wafted into the air as it began to come back solid.

After putting down his whip game, Ace removed the cooked crack from the coffee pot and placed it in the freezer to dry and harden. He pulled off dope-boy magic, stretching two zips enough to flip it into a four-and-a-split.

Once the work was all cooked up and bagged, Ace got himself dressed. He was rockin' a black Nike jogger suit with a huge red Nike logo stretched across the front of the zip-up hoodie and put on a pair of red AirMax 270's, which were fresh out the box. For accessories, he rocked his Cartier Buffalo frames, plus he strapped on his Kevlar vest beneath his jogger hoodie. After Ace was dressed, he tossed the four-and-a-half zips into a Nike drawstring bag and stuffed the foe-nickel in the pocket of his jogger pants with its stick hanging.

Ace left the crib and locked up. He made his way to his red Infiniti G35 parked curbside. As he entered the driver's side, he tossed the bag into the passenger seat. Before jumping into traffic, he texted his clientele to let him know he was on the way. It was nearly eleven am and Ace was out and about gettin' to the money.

Storming down Fond du Lac Avenue, Ace bobbed his head to the music. Turning onto a main street, he veered to the curb in front of a nice duplex house. He was there to make a serve to a teenage hustla. Once he texted he was outside, the hustla came out a moment later and entered the passenger's side of the whip, and he couldn't help but notice the blick in Ace's lap. Ace served the hustla the four-and-a-split of hard white in exchange for thirty-six-hundred-bucks. Afterwards, he and the young hustla parted company as Ace jumped back into traffic. He drove around town and made a few more serves before steering towards the hood.

Once he made it to the hood, he turned down the block and saw Sly standing on the front porch steps of their new trap spot. They'd made sure the new spot was secured with outside surveillance cameras so they could watch for any more raids.

Ace sped up then screeched to a stop at the curb and jumped out. Sly ran onto the porch and reached for his pistol, until he noticed it was only Ace there. Ace walked towards the spot, laughing. "Scary-ass nigga."

"Don't be doin' that shit. I almost popped the shit outta your ass, nigga," Sly told him.

"You didn't almost do shit. Whaddup tho?"

"Out here tryin' to stack some brick money."

Ace still hadn't been paid off for the kilo he fronted Sly. "Speakin' of, you, my nigga, so I ain't really sweatin' you over that cheese you still owe me for that brick. Just make sure you pay me that cheese whenever you got it."

"Say no more, my nigga. I got you," Sly assured.

Chedda stepped out of the spot with Bookie and Poppa in tow. They all shook up the rakes with Ace.

While the gang posted up, Ace was checking his news feed on Facebook. He saw Paris posted recent photos of herself with him and their son, Ace showed how much he loved his family by pressing "Like" on her post, and there was a video of Sonny Boy sitting inside his Audi SQ5 SUV, iced out and thumbing through a large stack of blue hundreds. Ace knew how much his homeboy was gettin' paid. Kiki posted some photos of her new hairdo, he pressed "Like" on her post.

Then there were people posting videos of Stone's funeral and typing statuses about what they assumed had happened to him and Star, some just wanted to know the true story. Ace smirked inwardly at the thought of how he had caught the pussy-ass nigga lackin'. He posted a status of his own, which read, "I woulda paid for the funeral, but he a opp."

"Y'all, check this shit out," Ace said, getting his boy's attention. "Mu'fuckas at that bitch-ass nigga, Stone's funeral right now."

"Let's slide through there and air that shit out," Poppa suggested. He stayed ready to bust.

"Nah. We gon' let his mama give him a proper burial," Chedda piped in. "Besides, now that Stone's ass is dead and gone, we ain't gotta worry about that nigga no more. So, we can focus on chasin' a bag."

"That's all that matters," Sly input.

Poppa sucked his teeth. "Speakin' of a bag, that nigga's shooters got you walkin' around in a damn shit-bag, big bro. And you talkin' about a proper burial. Man, fuck that!"

"Just look at the score, lil bro. We up on the body count right now," Chedda pointed out. After being popped up by some of Stone's shooters, Chedda had to wear a colostomy bag for the time being. However, at least he didn't get put in a body bag.

"Facts, Chedda is in a shit-bag, but he's still here with us, breathin'. Plus, we got some get back for Gee. Feel me?" Ace added. "Now there's other shit to think about. Like, what's goin' on with those cases you and Bookie caught."

Bookie let out a sharp breath. "Man, I'ont even wanna think about that shit. But the lawyer says he got our cases beat because twelve had raided the trap without a search warrant and no probable cause. And if the D.A. don't dismiss the charges against us, then we'll have to take that shit to trial." He and Poppa had drug and gun charges pending in court, due to being caught up in the unwarranted raid on their old trap spot that the crooked cop, Detective Lucas, had pulled off.

"We all know Lucas's crooked ass raided that trap hopin' to catch me in that bitch. But he ain't gon' never take me alive," Ace told them. Of the whole gang, the detective had it out most for Ace.

Chedda leaned back against the banister. "Dawg, fuck Twelve and opps. As long as we all make smart moves then we won't have to worry about gettin' indicted or murdered. Let all of these other niggas do the type of stupid shit that get 'em snatched up by the feds or popped up by their rivals. We just gon' keep gettin' to the money."

"I feel you on that, Chedda. But I ain't duckin' shit. 'Cause more money means more problems," Ace responded.

"That's why if we move smart, then the only problem we'll have to worry about is how to clean the money. And that's the reason we finna open the strip club." Chedda rubbed his palms together.

"Fa sho," Ace said. He slid his iPhone inside the front pocket of his joggers.

A neighborhood crackhead approached Poppa in the hopes of exchanging her food stamp Quest card for some crack. "How much food stamps on your Quest card, Auntie?"

"Two hundred dollars," the crackhead lady replied.

"I got you, Auntie. Here's an eight-ball." He figured they could always use some food in the trap spot. After the exchange, the crackhead scurried away to go and chase her first high.

16

Bookie caught a text on his iPhone and took a look at it. "Listen, I got these two J bitches at a hotel ready to suck 'n fuck right now. Y'all wanna pull up and flip 'em with me?"

"I'm with it," Poppa agreed.

"I'll leave them J's to y'all," Chedda said.

"I'm straight on that too," Ace seconded.

"What about you, Sly?" Bookie asked.

"Nah. You and Poppa go ahead. I'ma stay here and trap outta the spot," Sly answered. He turned for the house.

Chedda checked the time on his bust-down Rolly. "I'm finna get up outta here. I'll holla at y'all later."

"I'm about to do the same," Ace chimed in.

"Make sure y'all watch your backs in these streets, 'cause y'all know niggas wanna get their lick back over Stone. So, keep y'all poles close."

Poppa lifted his Gucci polo shirt just enough to show the butts of twin Glock .17s with extended clips on his waistline, and stated, "On Gee, niggas better be ready to shoot it out."

"No cap. And you know I'm poled up," Bookie input. "Pop, let's take your whip to meet up with those J's at the telly." He turned for the Lexus IS and Poppa followed.

Chedda shook his head. "Damn, Ace, you turned lil bro n'em into some fuckin' savages."

"Bro, that savage shit been in 'em, I just brought it out of 'em. Besides, we need niggas like them around us while we get money. It's good to know that lil bro n'em ain't scared to put in gun work," Ace replied.

"Just make sure they don't let them guns get in the way of gettin' money. Feel me?"

"Yeah, I feel you. Look, I'm finna dip. Hit my line if you need me."

Ace shook up with Chedda before they both entered their individual whips and went their separate ways. Noticing his gas tank nearly on E, Ace pulled into the gas station located on 27th and Capital Street, then parked at a gas pump. Once he pushed open the driver's door to step out the two iPhones and Glock that were in his lap fell onto the ground. Being that he was thinking about his next move, it had slipped Ace's mind the things were there in his lap. While some young trappers that were posted in front of the store observed, Ace picked up his shit. He stuffed the phones in the pocket of his Nike joggers, then placed the .45 on his waist with its stick protruding. As if nothing happened, he strolled towards the station, and when he approached the entrance, the young trappers called out they had weed and pills for sale.

When Ace walked into the station it was packed, with the line damn near to the back of the store. As the line started to shorten and Ace got closer to his turn at the register, all of a sudden, gunshots erupted outside.

Boom, boom, boom!

Prraat, prraat!

Instinctively, Ace ducked and upped his switch. As shots were exchanged between two random niggas, all the patrons ran for cover. The door flew open, and a nigga with a bullet wound rushed into the store, bustin' backwards over his shoulder outside, until his gun clicked empty. He hobbled to the back of the store, leaving a trail of blood, as the door flew open again with the assailant hurrying into the store after him. The assailant was bare chested with his shirt wrapped around his face, only exposing his eyes. And as he turned down the aisle where the wounded nigga was, he yelled, "Die, bitch-ass nigga!"

Prraat! Click, click...

The gun happened to jam up as the assailant squeezed its trigger and his victim dropped, clutching at the bullet wounds he suffered. The assailant gripped his pistol by its handle, grabbed his victim by the shirt and began repeatedly whipping him across the face. While the beating occurred, Ace replaced his blick on his waistline as he slipped out of the store then jogged to his Infiniti and hopped in.

Ace pulled off, getting away from the crime scene before twelve decided to show up. After witnessing how the scene unfolded back at the gas station, it made him realize just how easy it was for a nigga to get caught slippin' if he isn't on his toes. And he knew niggas were praying on his downfall, but thus far he was blessed enough to still be standing.

Back in traffic, Ace steered the foreign onto the highway, and he tore up the road in the fast lane as he rapped along to Key Glock's tune "Rich Blessed N Savage."

Chapter 3

Once Ace made it to the hood then stopped at the liquor store. While sitting in the parked Infiniti in front of the L-store, Ace had his pistol in lap with his trap-phone cradled in between his shoulder and ear as he was taking a call from a client about making a serve. He was too damn preoccupied to observe the nigga creepin' up on his whip.

"Nigga, run that shit!" a nigga growled and ducked his head into the open passenger window. Instinctively, Ace thought to go for his gun, that was until he realized it was a nigga from the hood named Cody, who busted out laughing. "Dawg, your ass should see your face right now!"

Ace shook his fuckin' head. "Cody, don't do no stupid shit like that again, 'cause I damn near blew your stupid ass down," he griped. Ace was always on edge due to all of the beef he had.

"Nigga, yeah right. You was sweet," Cody replied, still laughing.

"Whatever. Get the fuck away from my shit." Ace started to roll up the window.

"Hol' up. I wanna to holla at you real quick. I got a lick," Cody told him, wearing a grin with his chipped front tooth showing.

Ace halted rolling up the window and said, "A'ight. Hop in." He planted a hand on his blick as Cody entered the passenger seat. "So, whassup with this lick?"

Cody rubbed his palms together. "You heard about Rocco off the east side? He got some bricks of yae."

"I'm with it. If we can pull this off, we got a pile of shit."

"You know how this shit goes, it's either shoot or miss. I just pulled some shit off last night, I hit a heroin spot and dipped."

"Is this a job for the Glock, or a job for the Drac'?" Ace wanted to know. He didn't wanna run up in a spot unprepared.

"I'ont give a fuck, I'm just down for the take."

"But do you think we gon' make it out?"

"Shit, I ain't liable to say. Plus, I'ma have Mook with me. I'm slidin' with apes," Cody told him.

Ace didn't like the idea of another nigga in on the caper, especially Mook. "Fuck you need him for?"

"Just in case. Anyway, you know Peaches who fuck with Rocco?"

"Who, Lil Ray people?"

"Yeah. She said she seen Rocco outta town countin' at least a hunnit racks."

"I can't even cap, I need that money. Plus, the rent due, my son b-day and Christmas comin'."

Cody looked at him with hard eyes, and stated, "It don't look like you need that money as bad as me."

"Don't let looks fool you," Ace remarked. "Anyway, ain't that nigga, Rocco, goin' to court? I heard twelve booked him."

"They said that stupid nigga done served a narc. On top of that, he ain't go to his last court hearing, so I heard twelve lookin' for him."

"Shit, then we gotta hit this nigga ASAP."

"He gon' be home tonight, so that's where we gonna hit him," Cody laid out.

"I'm down," Ace replied. "Look, how 'bout we go and scoop up Mook, then we'll just ride around and smoke and kick it until tonight. That way we can come up with a game plan."

"Sounds like a plan to me."

"Cool. I'm finna go and grab some blunts real quick."

Before stepping out of the car, Ace pocketed his switch. He walked into the L--store and greeted Abdul, who was ringing up a neighborhood drunkard at the cash register. The drunkard paid for his cheap pint of Wild Irish Rose, then twisted off the bottle's cap and took a gulp of the hardcore liquor like it was only water. He strolled out the store, taking along his strong alcoholic odor. After purchasing a box of Backwoods, Ace made small talk with Abdul. As he turned to exit the store, there was Kiki and her pregnant-ass sister Red, making an entrance.

"Whassup with y'all?" Ace greeted the girls. He looked to Red, who avoided eye contact. "You don't fuck with me, huh, Red?"

"It ain't even like that, Ace," Red replied dryly.

"Listen, I know I shitted you in the past. But a nigga never meant to hurt your feelings." He knew Red was still mad at him because he had called her all types of hoes. Never again would he fuck bitches from his hood, because they were more like his sisters. "Hope we can be cool again, Red."

"We cool," she responded coolly before she moved along.

"Don't mind Red. She just been having contractions lately," Kiki told him. But she knew the truth was that Red was still mad at Ace for dissin' her. Kiki changed the subject. "Um, I see Cody outside in your car. His ugly ass had the nerve to try to shoot his shot at me. Please."

Ace chuckled. "Gee would turn over in his grave if you fuck with Cody, of all niggas."

"And he'd do the same if you fuckin' with Cody too," she replied, looking at him through slits. "Ace, you know his ass be out here robbing niggas and shit."

"Trust me, lil sis, I know how he gets down. But dawg ain't dumb enough to try no shit like that with a nigga like me."

Kiki snorted. "You giving Cody too much credit, 'cause his ass is as dumb as a doorknob."

"And, on Gee, he'll be as dead as one too if he try me," Ace swore.

"I bet." She knew how Ace was savage with his. "Enough about that nigga. I'ma need to re-up by tonight."

"I got some other shit I'ma be on tonight, so just hit my line sometime tomorrow and I'll pull up on you with somethin' extra. And I see you been gettin' your weight up too."

"A bitch gotta take care of herself in these streets, 'cause I don't wanna depend on no nigga for that."

"Respect. Just watch yourself, 'cause niggas don't give a fuck if you a bitch, they'll still run up on you if shit sweet."

"Bro, ain't shit sweet." Kiki patted her Prada handbag, letting Ace know she had her pistol concealed inside.

A grin spread on Ace's lips. "Say less. Look, just hit my line tomorrow."

"I will."

Ace gave her a hug before heading out of the store. As he approached the whip, he peeped Cody was wrapping up a phone call. Once Ace slid behind the steering wheel then he tossed the box of blunts and a sack of za into Cody's lap. "Roll up."

"Cool." Cody began rolling up a blunt.

"Now, let's go scoop up ya boy, Mook."

***

Later that night came quick. Ace had been waiting all day for this moment, it was time to hit the stash. He, Cody and Mook were sitting in the parked fiend rental down the alley behind Rocco's trap spot, because they didn't want to be seen on the outside surveillance cameras. For about a half-hour, they had been observing the place and peeped there was only one other person inside with Rocco. The game plan was for Ace to grab the paper and work while Mook went for the security tapes and Cody would watch their backs. Plus, Cody insisted that once they were sure to find the merch, he would murk Rocco since they were going in barefaced.

Ace looked over to Cody and then glanced through the rearview mirror at Mook, who he thought seemed 'noid. He checked his Glock, and introspectively said, *how these two actin', I shoulda came with my own niggas.* Instead, he asked, "Y'all niggas ready?"

It was about midnight when Ace knocked on the front door of the trap spot like a junkie, and the nigga that wasn't Rocco let him in. Ace peeped the nigga had a .40 in his hand. As soon as the nigga turned his back, Ace upped his own pole then slapped him over his head and the nigga dropped his gun like an amateur.

24

"If you move, bitch, I'ma damage you!" Ace growled, aiming his blick at the nigga's chest. A second later, the others barged in behind him.

"Where the mu'fuckin' work?" Cody demanded to know as he ran up on Rocco, who was seated on the couch looking stunned.

"It's in th-the kitchen!" Rocco cried out.

Cody jammed the barrel of his Glock .19 to Rocco's jaw, and hissed, "Your ass bet' not be cappin', or I'ma blow your shit out."

"Damn bro, I thought we was cool," Rocco said to Cody.

Cody struck him across the face with the pistol. "Hoe-nigga, you thought wrong. Now gimme all of your shit." He started strippin' Rocco of his possessions.

Mook stuffed his AK-47 to the other nigga's back, and demanded, "Take me to cut the damn cameras off." He was led into an adjacent room. While Ace left Cody to babysit the vic, he went in search of the stash. In the kitchen, he used the sleeve of his hoodie to rummage through the cabinets and cupboards only to find nothing. Then during the search, he discovered the bricks and some bundles of cash, all stashed away in the bottom drawer of the stove.

"You find that shit?" Cody called out from the front room.

"Yeah, found it," Ace called back. While he was tossing all of the merchandise inside the Nike drawstring bag, he heard a single gunshot and knew that as planned, Cody had whacked Rocco.

As the trio went for the back door, Ace noticed Mook started to panic. *I'm leavin' with this load 'cause I came way too far*, Ace contemplated. He peeped Cody and Mook trying to double cross him, but Ace was way too smart. So, he turned his gun on Mook and busted.

Boc, boc!

Ace hit Mook twice in the head, splattering his blood and brain matter all over some of the kitchen's cabinets and wall. Then he quickly turned his aim on Cody, and the two matched guns, Ace took two slugs in the Kevlar vest, which forced him stumbling backwards. But he popped Cody once in the throat and thrice in the torso, causing his body to drop to the tile floor with a thud.

Looking down at Cody's dead body, Ace said, "Good lookin', this shit came through." He knew there was no honor amongst thieves.

Ace hurried out the back door of the house full of dead bodies and ran down the dark alley to the fiend rental. As he jumped behind the steering wheel, he tossed the bag of merch into the passenger seat. He brought the engine to life and then stormed away from the crime scene. His mind was racing, and his chest hurt like hell from the impact where the slugs had struck his bulletproof vest, fortunately he had worn the body armor. He should've known the whole time Cody's true game plan had been to double cross him. But Ace was one step ahead of the game.

During the ride to his next destination, Ace stopped and dropped the murder weapon in the sewer. Once arriving at Savvy's crib, he parked the sedan curbside behind her Chrysler. Ace thought she was supposed to be working the club tonight. After grabbing up the drawstring bag from the passenger seat, he departed the whip and then made his way inside the crib. He found the place empty and figured that Savvy must have ridden to the club with her bestie, Nina.

In the bedroom, Ace tossed the bag onto the bed then shrugged out of the hoodie and took off the vest, both decorated with bullet holes. He lifted his T-shirt to examine himself and noticed there were bruises left on his chest caused by the bullets' impact, but at least he wasn't left riddled with bullets, like Cody and Mook.

Ace dumped all of the merch from the bag onto the floor and got down there and sat back up against the edge of the bed to figure out how much was his come up. First, he weighed up the soft white on a digital scale, it came out to some over a brick. Then he hand counted the paper-cheese, it came out to sixty-eight G's. Ace continued to get his money and weight up in the game the rich savage way.

Savvy entered the crib and found Ace in the bedroom with the money and drugs spread out on the floor. She shut the door behind herself and then sat her handbag on the dresser drawer, before kicking off her Air Force Ones near the bedside. "Ace, why do you have all that shit out like that?" she wanted to know.

"So, I can count it all up," Ace told her while wrapping a rubber band around one of the bundles of cash. "Ain't you s'pose to be at the club right now?"

"Yeah, but me and Nina decided to take off early because the night was slow." She took a seat on the edge of the bed beside where he sat on the floor.

"Bet it won't be a slow night when we open up our strip joint. That bitch gon' stay litty."

"Speaking of, I did get the chance to talk with Toucan tonight about the idea of having some of his girls work there."

Ace halted his task and gave her his undivided attention. "What'd that nigga say?"

Savvy smacked her lips. "His ass said he don't see a reason to have to do that when his girls are already making good money where they're working at right now. Unlike usual, he was acting like he didn't even wanna talk to me ever since you and him had some words. The nigga even had the balls to say I'd be better off if I wasn't fuckin' with you. So, I checked his ass and told him he don't even know you like that to even say anything about you. Then his ass got all mad and added some slick shit, talking about he don't gotta know you because he met your kind many times," she expounded with annoyance.

"Knew it was somethin' I ain't like about that dirty, mackin'-ass nigga. He just salty I got you and he don't. We don't need that nigga any fuckin' way, so don't even give his ass the time of day from now on. Fuck Toucan!" Ace huffed. "On some other shit, since you here, help me finish wrappin' up this paper."

"Or..." Sav lowered herself onto the floor and straddled his lap, then licked his neck. "How about I put this pussy on you?"

Ace gripped her phat ass in the skintight jeans she wore. "Sure you don't wanna give Toucan's soft-ass some of this pussy instead," he kidded.

"Dude, your black ass play too much." She playfully slapped his arm as he laughed. "I wouldn't even let that nigga eat this pussy."

"Lemme eat it."

"M'kay, Zaddy," Savvy said seductively as she started to help him out of his T-shirt.

"Ah, shit," Ace grunted in pain due to the soreness he suffered from the bullet's impact.

"You alright, Ace? How did this happen to you?" she asked out of concern once she saw the bruises on him.

"Didn't shit happen. I'm a'ight. Just make sure you report that .45 stolen," he responded coolly. He didn't want the bodies being traced back to her, since he had her buy the gun in her name. But Savvy knew he wasn't telling her what was up, seeing the bullet riddled body armor there.

Not giving Sav an opportunity to say any further words, Ace kissed her passionately. He pulled her fitted shirt over her head, his hands caressed her black lacy bra as he removed it and exposed her succulent titties. She planted her hands on his shoulders while he sucked on her pierced nipples. Pushing his head away, Savvy rose to her feet and stood her curvy frame right in front of him while he remained seated on the floor. Ace reached out and unbuttoned her jeans then watched with lust in his eyes as she slowly pulled them off, leaving on only her black lacy thong. Grabbing her at the waist, Ace pulled her pelvis close to his face, then used his fingers to push her panties to the side and began eating her pussy, while she had one foot propped up on the bed.

"Mmmm... Baby, this pussy tastes so damn yummy," Ace said sensually. He slipped two fingers deep inside her twat and sucked on her clit. Palming the back of his head, Savvy pushed his mouth onto her pussy.

"Damn, Ace... oooh... that shit feels... good," Sav moaned. She loved the way Ace was finger-fuckin' her slit and flicking his tongue over her clit at the same damn time. Tossing her head back, Savvy set free soft moans of pleasure as she felt herself reaching climax. "Yesss, I'm cummin'!"

Ace lapped up Savvy's cream. He then stood to his feet and French kissed her, and she tasted her own cum on his tongue. Sav pulled his jogger pants down around his AirMax, which he kicked off, then she pushed him back to sit on edge of the bed and straddled him. She peered into his eyes as she pushed her panties to the side and slid her slick pussy down on his throbbing dick.

He leaned back some while she bucked up and down on his lap, which caused her pretty titties to bounce. Gripping Sav's juicy ass cheeks in both hands, Ace rapidly lifted her up to the tip of his pipe and slammed her down onto its base. The pussy was so wet from having another orgasm, his dick slipped out of it a couple times, and she stuck his hardness back inside of her wetness then kept on riding him.

"Shit, boo, I'm finna fuck around and nut," Ace groaned, feeling himself growing close to releasing his seed. He remained seated on the edge of the bed as Savvy climbed down onto her knees and then lowered her sexy mouth onto his big dick. While Ace observed, she sucked his dick like there was a reward for it. Sav used her manicured hands to jack his saliva coated cock, while working her mouth on its tip and causing Ace's toes to curl. He squirted warm semen down her throat. "Sav, you suckin' a nigga dick so right!"

"A bitch like to treat you right," Savvy replied in a sexy tone. She arose then sat on his lap and pecked him on the lips. "I'm finna go and get in the shower."

"Go ahead. I'm finna finish wrappin' up this paper."

Ace slapped her on the ass as she started for the adjacent bathroom. He returned to wrapping rubber bands around the bundles of cash. Afterwards he put the merch from the lick in the stash spot with the rest of his shit. Ace was gettin' it how he lived, whether by robbing or drug money, and he was even willing to kill for it because he didn't have a problem with blood money.

Martell "Troublesome" Bolden

Chapter 4

Ace n'em had so many foreign whips parked in the gas station's lot, it looked like a car dealership. Over time, the gang had earned clout in the streets by way of checkin' a bag and steppin' on opps. It was hard not to notice them, because they moved through the city like BMF.

While Ace and Chedda were inside the station purchasing blunts and beverages, Bookie and Poppa were posted out front shootin' their shot at some bad bitches, and Sly was pumping gas into his whip. The whole gang was drippin' in designer 'fits and bust-down pieces around their necks and wrists but wasn't shit sweet with them because they were all poled up. They had just left Summerfest, one of the most popular festivals in Milwaukee. And after kickin' it at the fest, the gang was now on the way back to the hood.

When Ace and Chedda stepped out of the station, they posted near their whips with the rest of the gang. Some scantily dressed bitches twerked as Lil Baby's tune, "Get Money" banged from the speakers of Ace's whip. He pulled out his iPhone and went live on *Instagram*.

"What it do with y'all out there? Me and folks n'em just out here glazin' on shit." Ace turned the camera so the others could be seen standing behind him with their whips in the background. Chedda was smoking on a blunt of za, Bookie was spreading countless blue hundreds, Poppa was sandwiched between the bitches twerkin' their ass on him, and Sly was seated on the hood of his whip, rubbing his palms together. Grinning into the camera, Ace showed off the VVS stones in his mouth that matched those in his Cuban link chain, and added, "Y'all see how rich savages look."

"Niggas gettin' money over here, and we smokin' on that Stone pack," Chedda chimed in, then exhaled a thick cloud of smoke. Bookie threw some of the hundreds at the camera, and stated, "If you broke then you don't know!"

"And, on Gee, we ain't worried 'bout none of you poor-ass niggas bein' on some hatin' shit, 'cause we stay with at least thirty poppers on us." Poppa flashed his glizzy equipped with a thirty-shot stick.

"So, stay the fuck back, or get your shit pushed back," Sly input.

Plenty of hearts and comments were sliding up the side of the phone screen.

Ace positioned the camera onto himself, mugging through his Cartier Buffalo frames. "While you niggas and bitches out here playin' crazy, me and my savages playin' with a bag. And if you lookin' for us, we be in these streets so we ain't hard to find. I'm gone." He ended the live video.

The gang stood posted in front of the station for a little while longer. They chopped it up about how Summerfest had been lit. And the five of them passed the blunt around.

Ace turned and pulled open his car door, and said, "Let's get back to the hood. Last one there owes a rack."

"Bet," Chedda agreed.

Everyone hurried to their whips. Ace stepped into the peanut butter interior of his Infiniti G35, Chedda hopped into the leather guts of his Benz-Jeep, Bookie jumped into the bucket seats of his Audi Quattro, Poppa slid into the ostrich insides of his Lexus IS, and Sly climbed into the white inners of his Jag truck. They pulled out of the lot and into traffic, going well over the speed limit. Ace was in lead until Bookie dipped around a minivan. Sly tried staying in front of Chedda by blocking him each time he switched lanes. Poppa passed up Chedda and Sly as he gained on Ace and Bookie. As other motorists yielded for the yellow traffic light straight ahead, the gang zoomed through it. They were driving the foreigns like they were tryin' to wreck.

Once they reached the hood, Poppa was the first to pull up and park in front of the trap spot, followed by Bookie, then Chedda, then Ace, and finally Sly. The gang exited their whips and posted on the block.

"Y'all niggas can't fuck with my drivin' skills!" Poppa laughed.

"Pop, you cheated 'cause you went through the alley," Bookie protested.

"Only rule was not to be in last," Ace clarified.

"And since Sly was in last place, he owe Pop a G," Chedda pointed out.

"That shit light," Sly flexed as he fished a bankroll out of the pocket of his Gucci denim shorts. He counted out the debt owed, then paid up.

Ace was still waiting on Sly to pay up for the brick he fronted. "Sly, lemme holla at you over here real quick." He stepped away with Sly in tow.

"S'up, bro?" Sly asked.

"Listen, don't be talkin' 'bout shit light when you still owe me for that brick. You my boy and all, but I need mine. Feel me"

"Yeah, I feel you." On the low, Sly wasn't feelin' that shit. He didn't like how Ace was comin' at him but decided to let it be.

The two returned to the others.

"Y'all niggas good?" Chedda inquired.

"Yeah, we good. I was just hollerin' at bro 'bout some shit," Ace said coolly.

Poppa counted up his paper. "Y'all niggas wanna hit up the strip club tonight?"

"We ain't got time for that, 'cause we gotta flip the rest of the work," Bookie input.

"Matter fact, let's go and bag the rest of that shit up real quick," Sly suggested.

"Y'all niggas go ahead. I gotta get home to my bitch, 'cause her ass been blowin' up my line all fuckin' day," Ace told them.

Chedda piped in with sarcasm, "Which one of your bitches?"

"It ain't my fault that I'm lovin' both of my bitches the same. It's hard to explain, but they both in a tie."

"Dawg, you ain't shit."

"At least I ain't lie," Ace replied. "For the record, it's Paris who I'm finna go home to for the night. Savvy gotta wait."

"And speakin' of Sav, did you holla at her yet about gettin' some girls to audition at Baddies?"

"Yeah, I did. She said that ol' boy Toucan, who's pimpin' on the girls, talkin' about he don't need them workin' our club. And the peon-ass nigga had the balls to talk cash shit. Don't trip though. I know how we gon' get some bad bitches to show up at auditions."

"A'ight, bro. Look, I'ma get up outta here. I'll get at y'all later."

"Fa sho."

After shaking up with the rest of the gang, Ace and Chedda turned for their whips. The others made their way into the trap spot as Ace and Chedda drove off in separate directions.

Ace rode with the blick in his lap while keeping his eyes peeled for twelve and opps. He just wanted to be careful not to get caught lackin'. His iPhone vibrated while in the cupholder, he glanced down at it and noticed the caller was Sonny Boy. Turning the music down, he answered the call via Bluetooth.

"S'up, gang?" Ace asked as he yielded at a stoplight on 35th and Center Street.

"I'm good," Sonny responded. "Check it out. My brotha, Blue, just went live on *IG* with plenty niggas surroundin' him, all flashin' Dracos and switches, talkin' big shit about me and you."

"Fuck that's about?"

"Apparently, he saw you goin' live not too long ago, and he noticed you was rockin' the chain you took from Forty. Now Blue's talkin' 'bout he knows I must've sent you at the nigga."

Ace sucked his teeth, then remarked, "And, what?"

"And he sayin' you best give him the chain back ASAP, or he gon' take that shit back from you, and spin on me for sendin' you," Sonny informed. "Listen, I know my brotha, so I know he mean that shit."

"Sonny Boy, if your brotha want his dead-ass nigga's chain, then he can buy this mu'fucka back for thirty G's. 'Cause let's keep shit one-hunnit, since Blue already know we had somethin' to do with Forty gettin' smoked, he plans on beefin' with us any fuckin' way. I know that's your brotha and all but on Gee, if dawg try somethin' then his ass betta down me, or I'ma shoot his mu'fuckin' brains out," he forewarned assertively. Noticing Paris calling on the other line, Ace swiped "Ignore" on her call.

Sonny knew that not only was Ace dead serious, but he was also right. "Ace, Blue my brotha, but I'll never change on you like how he did me, once I didn't give his ass more cash than he expected when first got out the feds. That nigga didn't show no fuckin' loyalty over royalty. So, it is what it is. Just keep your pole close," he expressed emphatically.

"Needless to say, I keep my shit on me at all times when I'm slidin' through the trenches," Ace assured.

"No doubt. Look, lemme get back to the money. Plenty much love, my boy."

"Never enough."

Ace ended the call as he pulled off with traffic once the light flipped green. He couldn't help but think about the shit he and Sonny Boy had just rapped about concerning Blue. One thing for sure, Ace wasn't duckin' no smoke. But he would be on the lookout for Blue, because he knew the nigga would try to pull up on him eventually. Ace thought, *if Blue try to take this chain, then his ass better take my life along with it.*

Arriving at his crib, Ace pulled to the curb and parked behind Paris's Eclipse. He grabbed his phone then pocketed his blick before hopping out the foreign whip and stepping towards the front door. Once Ace entered, he trailed his way into the master bedroom and found Paris in bed on her iPhone, scrolling through *TikTok*, while Adonis was asleep beside her.

"Look who finally decided to bring his ass home," Paris spoke sarcastically. She turned on the lamp positioned on the nightstand at her bedside.

Ace sat his phone atop the dresser and then placed his Glock inside the top drawer. "Paris, don't even start trippin' and shit."

"Dude, you're the one trippin' by not answering any of my texts or calls all day, then coming home late like it's all good."

"I was tied up all day," he deceived.

"Probably was with some bitch," she accused.

"Man, I ain't finna do this with you tonight. I'ma hop in the shower and then take my ass to sleep," he told her as he headed for the adjacent bathroom.

"What the fuck ever, Ace," Paris huffed.

Subsequent to taking his shower, Ace returned to the room and got in bed. Paris laid with her back to him with their son in between them, and he knew she was heated at him. Ace had it in mind to make it up to her as he dozed off.

Chapter 5

Once Ace awoke in the morning, he rolled over in bed and found Paris lying beside him, scrolling through his phone. "Fuck is you doin'?" he questioned.

"Who in the hell is Savvy?" Paris demanded to know, ignoring his question. He reached for the phone and Paris held it away as she sat up in bed. "Answer me, Ace. Who is Savvy?"

"Just a bitch who was hired to work at our club. Now gimme my damn shit." Ace grabbed his phone from her hand.

"Then why is the bitch texting you, calling you Daddy and sending heart-eyes emojis, if she just works at the club?"

Ace swung his feet onto the floor and sat up on edge of the bed with his back to her. "Man, it ain't even like that."

"Ace, are you fuckin' the bitch? Huh?"

Ace thought about his answer a moment. "No, Paris, I ain't fuckin' the bitch. Happy now?" he said with a hint of sarcasm.

Paris stepped out of bed and made her way around then stood in front of him. "Lemme find out, Ace. I'ma fuck you and that bitch up."

"If your ass wasn't goin' through my shit and bein' so damn nosey, we wouldn't even be havin' this problem right now."

"No nigga, if your ass wasn't always running the streets, then I wouldn't have a reason to go through your shit, and we wouldn't even be having this problem," Paris remarked as she made her way into the adjacent bathroom and then slammed the door shut behind her.

Ace could hear Paris still talking shit from inside the bathroom. Part of him wanted to tell her ass the truth but he knew that would come with baby mama drama. Instead of having to hear her mouth, Ace decided he would get dressed and bounce. He put on the same 'fit he had rocked the day before. Paris exited the bathroom and saw him getting dressed.

"Dude, where you finna go?" she wanted to know.

As Ace pulled on his shirt, he said, "To my sis crib." He headed into the bathroom.

"Then take your son with you so he can play with Breon, if that really is where your ass is going."

"Man, just get him ready, instead of tryin' to be so damn sarcastic," he mumbled while brushing his diamond filled teeth.

Paris went to get Adonis dressed. *I got something for Ace ass, since he thinks he's so damn slick,* she mused bitterly. Seeing those texts from some other bitch had Paris so upset. But she couldn't exactly say whether or not he was cheating on her. One way or another, she was going to find out.

After Ace collected everything he needed, he grabbed his son and headed out to the Infiniti. He opened the driver's door and put his son inside, who climbed over the middle console into the passenger seat. Then Ace slid behind the steering wheel. He push-started the whip and then pulled off down the street.

Soon thereafter, Ace pulled up in front of Mika's crib and parked. He saw she was seated on the front porch steps, along with Kiki and Red, while Bookie and Poppa were posted up on the block, and Reverend Johnson sat watching the neighborhood from his front patio. The summer sun was beating down on the city, it was so hot outside that someone had busted open the fire hydrant so the residents could cool off in the showering water. The hood was always goin' down. Once Ace and Adonis got out of the car, Adonis ran off to play with Breon, and Ace approached Mika n'em.

"S'up with y'all?" Ace greeted the trio of girls.

"Hey, lil bro," Mika said. "I just got off the phone with Paris talking about you."

"'Bout what?" he inquired.

"About how your ass always running the streets and shit."

"I just be doin' my thang. I'ont even know why her ass stay trippin'."

"Because that girl isn't stupid, Ace. She's not wrong for thinking you're out here creeping on her with these little nasty-ass bitches—no offense, Red. Anyway, Paris told me about that girl Savvy texting you, and I remember you bringing that girl over here before. My point is that a woman's intuition is almost always right. And y'all niggas are so messy that y'all always get caught," Mika laid out.

Ace had to admit his sista was on point. "Whatever, sis. I ain't worried about gettin' caught up."

"Then that's on you," Mika replied. She yelled at the boys to stop throwing rocks at cars, then returned her attention to Ace. "Bro, your son is bad as hell. He gets that shit from you."

"Paris always says the same thing. I can't wait 'til Mama touch down, so she'll be able to bond with him," Ace replied.

"I have no doubt she'll love his bad ass. And when she do get out, we gotta make sure she feels at home. I'll have all of my things moved out of this house by next week, then we can fix it up for Mama."

"I'll do whatever needs to be done to look out for her."

Their mother, Gale, was about to be released from federal prison in a matter of weeks after spending the past six years in lockdown. Ace and Mika wanted to give her all of the love and support she would need.

While Ace n'em were posted out on the block, an ice cream truck came down the street with its happy tune sounding from the loudspeaker. All of the ghetto children ran towards the truck, including Adonis and Breon. Ace took it upon himself to wave down the truck, he pulled out a bankroll and slipped a C-note to the serviceman.

"Make sure you give everybody what they want until that hunnit is spent. And lemme get a ice cream sammich," Ace told the serviceman. As Ace stepped away after receiving his ice cream sandwich, he heard all the kids shouting out their requests for different flavored ice creams and popsicles. Ace stepped back over to Mika n'em while eating on his treat, and said, "If y'all want somethin' from the ice cream truck then go and get it."

"Ooh, I'm finna go and get me one of those Choco-tacos," Kiki said and headed towards the truck with Red.

Ace gave his big sis the remaining half of his ice cream sandwich before making his way over to Bookie and Poppa, who were standing under the shade of the tree that was decorated with

Gee's shrine. Gee was missed every day and his family and friends would do their all to represent him and keep his name alive. Ace and some of the others from the hood had gotten a portrait of Gee tattooed on them in his memory, including Kiki. And in his honor, they even dubbed the block they had all grown up on, and would more than likely die on, "Gee Street."

"Whassup, lil bros?" Ace said as he approached them.

"Me and Pop just thinkin' about all of the shit we did with Gee," Bookie answered.

Poppa shook his fuckin' head. "Man, I miss my dawg."

"Yeah, me too." Ace had to admit gettin' revenge for Gee felt good, but it still hurt that he was dead and gone. "I remember seein' all three of y'all runnin' around here bustin' windows and sweatin' me for dollars, then all of a sudden, y'all started bustin' poles and gettin' money with me." He chuckled. "It's crazy how everything changed. And now I'ont got my lil bro no more."

"Big bro, just know you still got us," Poppa told him.

"That's on Gee," Bookie cosigned.

"No doubt." Ace knew Boo and Pop was down for him, but he didn't want them losing their freedom or lives on his behalf. Instead, he wanted to see them make it out the trenches. "Listen, opps out here killin' real niggas, man, the streets have gotten crazy. Don't get me wrong, I'll never let a nigga play me 'cause I gotta eat, that's on Gee. But y'all young niggas need to find another way out 'cause the streets won't save y'all. Feel me?" he expressed.

"Ace, you always givin' us jewels," Bookie heeded.

"Facts. But this shit in us," Poppa input.

Ace understood. "Y'all just do whatever it takes to stay free and alive in these streets."

"Fa sho," Poppa assured.

While standing there, they all peeped the BMW 745 as it made its way down the block. The pearl white Beamer sittin' on chrome rims pulled curbside and parked across the street from Mika's place. Mika's boyfriend, Money Mel, stepped out the whip dripped in ice on his neck and wrists. Ace noticed how Bookie and Poppa clutched their sticks and mean-mugged Mel as he stepped on the sidewalk. Mel acknowledged Ace with a nod of the head and Ace returned it.

"Chill, lil bros. Dawg good," Ace let them know.

"Fuck is dawg?" Pop asked.

"Sis fuck with him. His name Money Mel. Apparently, he's ballin' hard."

Boo admired Mel's drip. "Shit, with all of that water on the nigga's neck and wrists, he gotta be a baller."

"Matter fact, he was just in the feds with the big homie, Baller. I'ont know Mel like that, however if Baller fuck with the nigga, then he must be real. Plus, since Mika with the nigga, I'ma give him the benefit of doubt. But if he turn out to be a fuck-nigga, then on Gee, I'ma treat his ass," Ace stated. His iPhone chimed, indicating that he had received a text. Pulling his phone out, Ace checked its display and saw the message was from Savvy, and he read it.

SAVVY:
Hey, Daddy. I need to see u.
It's important.

Ace thought about Paris reading Savvy's messages earlier. He texted her back in response.

ACE:
I'll be there to see u in a min.
And it better be important like
you say.

"Lil bros, I'm finna slide. I'll holla at y'all." Ace shook up with the two, then went and asked Mika to look after his son for a little bit before he headed towards his foreign. He opened the driver's door then as Ace slid behind the steering wheel he waved at the Rev, who waved back. Ace pulled off down the street and drove under the water cascading from the fire hydrant as he went on his way.

During the ride, Ace thought about the shit Mika had said about him fuckin' with Savvy behind Paris's back. Though Paris was his wifey and Savvy was his sidepiece, he was loving both of his bitches the same. Arriving at Savvy's crib, Ace veered to the curb and parked the Infiniti. He sent Sav a quick text to inform her that he was outside. A moment later, she emerged from the house and Ace peeped that she was looking good, wearing only a fitted baby T-shirt, pair of coochie cutter shorts and fuzzy slippers, with her hair and nails done. She made her way to the car then entered its passenger seat.

Suddenly, a black Benz SUV braked to a hard stop beside the Infiniti. Instinctively, Ace grabbed the pipe from his lap and was ready to bust, until he noticed Paris jumping out of the passenger side of the SUV, which he finally realized belonged to Chedda's baby mama, Antoinette. Before Ace could react, Paris tried snatching open his door but found it locked.

"Unlock this fuckin' door, Ace!" Paris demanded while banging on the driver's window with her closed fist. "I knew your dawg-ass was in these streets cheating on me."

"Paris, calm your ass down. You trippin' for no fuckin' reason," Ace shouted. A little too late, he realized that earlier when she had his phone, she must have turned on his location app in order to track his every move to try to catch him stepping out on her.

"Open the door so I can beat that bitch ass!"

"Boy, you best get that crazy bitch. Whoever she is got me fucked up," Savvy warned.

"That's my BM. Don't trip, I'ma handle her," Ace assured.

Paris picked up a large rock and busted the driver's window. "Get the fuck out the car, now!"

"Paris, what the fuck you doin'?" Ace hopped out the car and Paris hit him with a flurry of fists. He snatched her up and restrained her. "Chill the fuck out and listen, dude. What your ass doin' out here followin' me any fuckin' way?"

"Because you won't tell me the truth, so I had to find out for my-damn-self. Is this the bitch who was texting you, Ace?"

"'Paris, why don't you take your ass back home and we'll talk when I get there," Ace told her as he ushered her to the SUV.

"Nigga, get your hands the fuck off me!" Paris yanked herself free of his grasp.

"C'mon, friend, let's go. Now you know what his ass been doing," Nett said from the driver's seat. "Ace, you so damn wrong."

Paris got all up in his face. "You know what? Don't bring your ass home tonight. Stay with that bitch," she cried, using her index finger to push his forehead with each syllable. "And don't worry about Adonis because I'm finna go and pick him up now." No more words, Paris jumped in the SUV and then Nett drove off.

Ace knew he had to make shit right with Paris some way. But he would give her ass some time to cool off, because he didn't want to make shit worse than it already was. However, she was gonna have to accept her position in his life without the insecurities.

"Now what, Ace?" Savvy asked. She was now standing outside the car.

"Now I'ma just let her ass know what it is," Ace answered. "You just keep playin' your position."

Sav smacked her lips. "Make sure you clean that mess up with your wifey," she replied flippantly.

"Bitch, shut up with that shit. Any fuckin' way, what's so damn important that you wanted to see me, huh?" he wanted to know.

She stood with her arms folded and her weight shifted to one side. "I know this may not be what you wanna hear right now, especially with your baby mama drama, but I'm pregnant."

"You sure?"

Savvy scoffed. "Yeah, I'm sure. I was late on my period, so I went the clinic today. I'm four weeks along."

Ace couldn't believe this shit. First, Paris had just caught him with another bitch, and now if she was to find out Savvy is carrying his baby, Paris would fuck him up. He didn't want to make shit worse than it already was. Besides, he had never seen himself having no kids with Savvy.

"Sav, I ain't feelin' that shit," Ace told her, keepin' it real.

"Well, you don't have to worry because I also wanted you to know I scheduled for an abortion. Truth is, I'ont got time to be walking around pregnant. But now I know how you really feel," Savvy remarked and shook her damn head.

"Least I ain't lie," was all he could say as she turned for the house.

Ace pulled open the driver's door and then used his hand to brush the shattered glass out of the seat. He stepped in and set off on his way to Shane's car shop in order to have his busted-out window replaced.

Chapter 6

While Ace stood in front the trap spot, a fiend approached him looking to cop some dope, but Ace was beyond his nickel and dimin' days, so he directed the fiend to one of the pack-boys posted up on the block. He was with Chedda, and they were shooting the breeze.

"Dawg, my OG comin' home from the feds next month," Ace said.

"That's good. Haven't seen her since we were young teens. I remember back then we used to steal some of her weed, and she didn't notice 'cause she had so many pounds of it."

"Yeah, Mom's always been a hustla like that. I just wish she would've been there for me and my siblings more. But we past that shit. Now I just wanna make sure she good and don't need for nothin'," Ace expressed.

"I feel you. All you can do is be there for her as much as you can," Chedda told his boy.

"Fa sho." Ace's iPhone rang. Pulling the phone out of the pocket of his Amiri cargo shorts, Ace checked the display but didn't recognize the number. *Fuck is this*? he wondered as he answered the call. "Who dis?"

"S'up, homie. This Money Mel. Got your number from Mika," he replied.

"A'ight. Whaddup?"

"A nigga tryin' to cop some of that smoke you got on deck. Want a zip of that shit."

"I got that. Just pull up by my sis crib," Ace told him.

"Cool. I was on the way there now to see her anyway. Plus, I need to holla at you about some shit," Mel said.

"Say no more." Ace ended the call. He looked to Chedda, and said, "Let's walk around the corner to sis crib real quick."

"Who was that?" Chedda wanted to know as he walked with Ace.

"'Member the nigga Money Mel I told you about, who I met through Mika?"

"The one nigga who you said was in the feds with Baller, right?"

"Yeah. That was just him. He wanna cop some smoke, and he said he need to holla at me 'bout some shit."

"Holla at you 'bout what?"

"He didn't say. I'ma have to see whassup when he pull up to Mika's crib."

"So, Mika fuck with that nigga the long way now?"

"I guess so. She told me he treats her and my nephew good, so I'm cool with it. Plus, the nigga seem like he a real one."

Making it around the corner to Mika's crib, Ace and Chedda took a seat on the front porch steps. They sat there awaiting Money Mel to arrive. While waiting, Ace made sure the weight on the ounce of weed was proper, he didn't need a scale because he could eyeball the work.

It wasn't long before Money Mel's BMW 745 came cruising down the block and pulled to the curb, then parked across the street from Mika's crib. Mel pushed the driver's door open then stepped out, he was drippin' in designer attire from head to toe and his neckwear and timepiece was bust-down with diamonds. Plus, the .40 Glock equipped with a thirty-shot stick that protruded from his waist couldn't go unnoticed. Mel made his way across the street and approached Ace and Chedda.

Ace stood up and said, "What's poppin'? This my nigga, Chedda. And that's Money Mel." He introduced the two so there wouldn't be any awkwardness and they acknowledged one another. "Here's the zip. Just gimme a buck fifty."

"Cool." Mel fished out a bankroll then peeled off the fee in exchange for the ounce. He lifted the sandwich bag full of weed to his nostrils and inhaled its strong odor. "Damn. This shit smells musty!"

"I got pounds of that shit if you ever wanna cop some. And I'll show you love on the price since you fuck with my big homie, Baller."

"I'ma most definitely cop some pounds of this shit from you," Mel assured. "But speakin' of Baller, that's what I need to holla at you about. Had my lil cousin, who's still locked up in the same fed prison with him, do a background check on you, and Baller says you're valid. No disrespect, just had to make sure your name is good in these streets if I'ma fuck with you. Feel me?"

"Yeah, I feel you. But if that's all you had to holla at me about, then you coulda told me that on the phone."

"Too much talkin' on the phone is how the feds book niggas. Plus, there's more to it. Baller wanted me to let you know some nigga from his gang ratted him out, nigga named Phat."

"Phat? Yeah, I know that nigga. I ain't surprised, 'cause me and my dawg here been skeptical about his ass lately any fuckin' way," Ace replied with disgust.

"Knew somethin' was up with him," Chedda input. "I never trusted Phat, which is why I always advised you not to fuck with him, Ace. Niggas like him won't hesitate to get you outta the way if it benefits 'em."

Mel leaned back up against the banister, and reported, "Baller said that nigga had fucked around and got jammed up with a few bricks, and instead of takin' his hit, he gave up Baller in exchange for his freedom. It's all in Baller's paperwork. So, I'm sure his ass is still workin' with the feds."

Ace scoffed. "Say no more. I ain't goin' out like Baller."

The front door came open and Mika stepped onto the porch. "Why are y'all out here on the porch? Come inside."

"Me and Chedda about to head back around the corner to the spot," Ace told her. "Money Mel, good lookin' on that info."

"I got you."

"Just hit me up whenever you wanna shop with me."

"Fa sho."

As Ace and Chedda started on their way, Mel followed Mika into the house.

"What we gon' do about this shit with Phat's rat ass?" Chedda wanted to know.

"We gon' make sure that nigga get handled," Ace answered. "Can't let his ass get away with snitchin' on Baller. Plus, I'ont need Phat willin' to snitch on me too." He realized Phat had more than enough dirt on him to use as a get-out-of-jail-free card, and that troubled him. Now Ace had to plot on Phat.

"How we gon' do that?"

"Don't trip, I know exactly how." Ace pulled out his phone and dialed up Sonny Boy.

"What it do, Ace?" Sonny answered.

"Listen, I need to holla at you ASAP 'bout somethin'.'"

"Sounds like somethin' is up. Is it about Blue?"

"Nah, this ain't about Blue. Right now, it's about Phat. Some shit I need to holla at you 'bout face-to-face. Where you wanna meet up?"

"A nigga hungry as fuck right now, so we can meet at Denny's located on Mill Road."

"I'll be there in a min." Ace ended the call. He looked to Chedda, and said, "That's how we gon' handle Phat."

"How you figure that?" Chedda asked.

"'Cause Phat pulled some fuck shit on Sonny Boy a couple weeks back with some work. Sold him some dope that had been danced on too much. And I'm sure Sonny want some get-back for that shit. Plus, once I let him know that Phat bitch-ass is a rat, then I know he gon' want that nigga dead too, 'cause Phat got a lot of dirt on him also. So, it's best for us all that we smoke the fat ass nigga," Ace explained.

"Then let's do what we gotta do to exterminate Phat the rat," Chedda input. He switched topics. "So, who the fuck is Blue?"

"Sonny's brotha. Damn, I forgot to let you know whassup with that nigga. A while back, Sonny Boy had an issue with Blue and his right-hand man named Forty. We damn near had to air them niggas out at the club one night. Anyway, Sonny put me onto Forty, so I stripped the nigga for his Cuban link and left him stiff. Now Blue figured out me and Sonny had somethin' to do with the shit after he saw me goin' live on the '*Gram* rockin' the chain. And he posted a video sayin' I best give him Forty's shit back, or he gon' spin on me and Sonny. I'm like, he can buy it back, or else. Feel me? That's whassup with Blue."

Chedda shook his damn head because Ace was always into something. "Ace, just be on point out here. You already know I'm down for whatever."

"Fa sho."

Once Ace and Chedda were back around the corner at the trap spot, they loaded into Ace's Infiniti. Ace zipped through traffic while Chedda rode shotgun as Baby Money's track, "Two Strikers" played in the background.

Chedda's phone chimed, indicating he had received a text, so he read it. Afterwards, he looked to Ace and told him, "Fam, drop me off at my crib so I can see what Nett wants. Her ass talkin' 'bout she needs me."

"Can't it wait 'til we get done hollerin' at Sonny Boy?" Ace questioned.

"Just drop me off and then you can go and holla at him your-self. Afterwards you can swing back by then let me know how shit went. I need to make sure my bitch and kids are good."

"A'ight." Ace respected that Chedda was all about taking care of his family first. He thought that's what a real nigga should do. "Speakin' of, so, my nigga, whassup with you and Paris? Nett told me y'all still ain't talkin'," Chedda brought up.

Ace let out a sharp breath. "Man, I tried callin' and textin' her ass but she ain't answer. So, I ain't been to the crib in damn near three days now. Low key, I miss my bitch and son. I hate she caught a nigga like that," he admitted.

"Then nigga, why don't you take your ass home to 'em? I bet Paris act all mad at you, but on the inside she gon' be happy as hell to see you. Her ass still love your dirty drawers, from what she's been tellin' my bitch."

"I ain't gon' lie, when Paris and Nett pulled up on me while I was with Sav, I was sick with it."

"And you already know ever since your fool-ass got caught up with that bitch, my BM has been on my ass 'cause she afraid I'm in these streets doin' the same. On the low, Nett damn near don't want a nigga kickin' it with you no more. Well, I told her to gone with that shit, 'cause no matter what, you my bro. But I can't have you fuckin' up my relationship, so your ass gon' have to go home today and straighten shit out with Paris," Chedda expounded.

Ace chuckled. "I know Nett told your scary-ass to holla at me, so don't act like this was all your idea. A'ight, I'll go see Paris today."

"Good."

Following the detour to Chedda's crib to drop him off, Ace arrived at Denny's. Soon as he was pulling into the parking lot, he spotted Sonny Boy's Audi truck and Ace parked beside it in the vacant spot. He figured Sonny must have just made it to the location himself, because he was just stepping out from his whip. Ace stepped out of his own whip, then made his way around its trunk and approached Sonny Boy.

"Been sittin' here for 'bout twenty mins waitin' on you," Sonny made him aware. He took a pull on the remainder of the blunt of weed he was smoking.

"My bad. Had to drop off my nigga, Chedda, so he could deal with some shit," Ace responded.

Sonny leaned back up against his vehicle. "It's cool. Now, whaddup with the shit you need to holla at me 'bout, pertainin' to that nigga, Phat?" He was eager to know the news.

"'Member I told you I been gettin' funny vibes from buddy? Well, turns out his ass on some funny business."

"You mean like snitchin'?"

"Straight like that. Just got word from my big homie, who's in the feds, that Phat was the one who had dropped a dime on him. More than likely, it means that police-ass nigga is still workin' with them people. And I'ont know about you, but I ain't comfortable with lettin' his ass live, knowin' he got some dirt on me," Ace laid out.

Sonny puffed the blunt and then passed it to Ace. He understood where Ace was coming from, because the thought of Phat having dirt on him also didn't sit well with him either, and Sonny wasn't willing to be anyone's scapegoat. "A'ight. That nigga gotta go. So, how we gon' play this?"

50

"We gon' backdoor Phat's stupid ass. You call that nigga like it's for a re-up, that way we can also take his shit. Just make sure you have him meet you someplace where no witnesses will be around and then we'll wipe his nose."

"And what about his two shooters, Troy and Nice? Them niggas always with him whenever he makes plays."

Ace puffed the blunt, then exhaled thick smoke and could tell it was some of the weed he had on deck. "Fuck them niggas. We gon' blow 'em down before they see it comin'. Just be ready to bust."

"Say less. When you wanna get down on this snitch-ass nigga?" Sonny wanted to know.

"Give it a couple days, so we can find a low-key place to do this shit."

"Bet. I'ma keep in touch with you on that. Listen, I done lost my fuckin' appetite talkin' about this ol' bitch-ass nigga, so I'ma catch up with you later," Sonny Boy said. He shook up the forks with Ace before returning inside his whip.

Once the two parted ways, Ace headed back to Chedda's crib to update him. He pulled to the curb and texted Chedda to let him know he was outside. Moments later, Chedda came out and then slid into the passenger seat.

"Shit all good with the Fam?" Ace inquired.

"Yeah. Nett just wanted me to come check in on her and the girls," Chedda told him. "Anyway, how'd the meet go with Sonny Boy?"

"He's down to back door Phat. Now all we gotta do is figure out the time and place."

"The game is cold but it's fair."

In the game, snitching goes against the code. And by not stickin' to the code, niggas was fuckin' up the game by working with the alphabet boys, instead of taking their hit. And Ace was more than ready to take Phat out for being a snitch-ass nigga, because it was part of the game.

"Bro, I'ma get up with you later. Lemme take my ass home to Paris and my son."

"Go and handle your business, Fam."

The two shook up, then Chedda stepped out of the car and Ace drove off on his way. During his ride home, Ace thought about what he would say to Paris as he played PNB Rock's tune, "My Bad." Of course, he understood how bad he had fucked up, he needed to straighten shit out with her. Now he realized just how wrong he was for thinking what she didn't know wouldn't hurt her when came to him fuckin' with Savvy. And to add insult to injury, he had gotten Sav pregnant. Fortunately for him, Paris didn't know that much, and on top of it, Savvy was willing to proceed with having an abortion.

Although Sav was willing to get the procedure done, Ace could tell she was hurt by his initial reaction once she had informed him of her pregnancy. As much as Ace genuinely cared about Savvy, he knew it was in everyone's best interest that she abort the baby before it was too late. Ace would make it up to Sav some way, but at the moment he needed to focus on making up with Paris.

Ace soon arrived at the crib and parked behind Paris's Porsche truck. He grabbed up his phone and texted Paris to come outside, she left his ass on read. As he was finna step out of the car, to his dismay, Paris emerged from the front door of the house. She took a seat on the porch steps and Ace departed the whip then approached her. He tried to offer her some affection, but she just wasn't in the mood, so she pushed him away.

"Damn, it's like that?" Ace uttered.

"Boy, you made it that way," Paris remarked with an apparent attitude.

"You right about that. Listen, I get why you mad at me, and that's my bad. But I need for you to understand you my wifey, and ol' girl is just—"

"Do you wanna be with the bitch?" Paris intervened, leering at him with cutting eyes.

Ace shook his head. "No, I'ont wanna be with her. If I did, then I wouldn't be here tryin' to kiss your ass right now. Paris, a nigga wanna be with you and our son. You know how much I love the shit outta y'all."

Paris scoffed. "Whatever, dude. You for the streets."

He sat beside her on the steps, and she scooted away from him some. "I know I be in these streets a lot, but I also know that home is right here with you and Adonis. Bae, don't sit here and act like you don't want my ass at home with y'all," Ace expressed.

"And you don't sit here acting like I'm supposed to just welcome you back home with a damn smile, Ace. You lucky I'm tired of your son asking me where his daddy at, or I wouldn't even consider the thought of it," Paris remarked.

"Paris, I'm just tryin' to be home with you and my son, at least for the night."

In that moment, Adonis came outside while wearing only his briefs and a stained T-shirt. "Hey, Daddy!" he cried out happily and ran over to Ace, who sat Adonis in his lap. "You staying home with me and Mommy?"

Ace didn't exactly know how to answer that, so he looked to Paris, who coarsely said, "Mm-hm, Daddy staying home. But his ass will be sleeping in your bed with you."

"Yaae! Daddy sleeping with me!" Adonis exclaimed, not understanding that his mom and dad was having grownup problems. He was just excited that daddy was home.

Paris rose to her feet and went inside with Ace carrying their son as he followed. Ace understood that Paris would make it hard on him to get back in good graces with her. However, he would do what it takes. Also, he realized she wouldn't trust him as much for a while. All he could do was allow her to be mad for the time being, but he had no doubt they could work it out. For he knew Paris loved him, no matter the amount of clout or cash he had, unlike the streets.

Chapter 7

It had been two days since Ace was back home with his girl and son. He hadn't stepped out into the streets much, because he wanted to make shit right with Paris, although she was still mad at him. However, Ace cared to make things better. And as mad as Paris still was, she did like having Ace at home for a change. Also, she realized the effort he was putting forth to fix things between them, although she still wasn't quite ready to trust him again. Trust was gained in drops and lost in buckets.

It was evening and the family had just gotten done eating dinner. Paris was in the kitchen tidying up and Ace was in the living room watching a Milwaukee Brewers baseball game, while Adonis was there playing with some of his toys. They were enjoying being in each other's presence.

Ace's iPhone vibrated, he grabbed it from the end table and saw it was a call from Chedda. "Whassup?"

"Step outside real quick so I can holla at you," Chedda said.

"A'ight."

Ace went to let Paris know he would be right outside with Chedda for a moment, and when he attempted to give her a kiss, she turned her head in denial. He went ahead and stepped outside, where he made his way to Chedda's Benz-Jeep and entered the passenger side. The two shook up the rakes.

"I see wifey got your ass on a short leash," Chedda half-joked. He sipped from the soda bottle of red syrup, then passed it to his boy.

"You know how shit be when a nigga get caught up in his doggish ways," Ace replied with a chuckle. He sipped the high-tech, then made the mad face. "Damn, that shit strong!"

"I know, right? Anyway, how's shit between you and Paris so far?"

Ace let out a heavy breath. "Fam, her ass is still mad as hell at me. She won't even let me touch her, talkin' 'bout I probably got cooties from the other bitch." Chedda laughed, and Ace told him, "That shit ain't funny, my nigga."

"My bad, bro. The shit is funny though. Who knows what Savvy got."

"Trust me, Sav don't got shit. She's been blowin' me up too." Ace turned the drank up to his lips for a sip before placing it in the cupholder.

Chedda shook his damn head. "Dawg, you still didn't learn your lesson? Just don't let Paris find out."

"Don't even worry about me and Paris, I'ma straighten it out," Ace said, sure of himself. "Anyway, what you wanna holla at me about?"

"Nothin' much. I just wanted to check in on you since your ass been cooped up in the crib for a couple of days now. Also, I thought you could use a break away from wifey."

"Good lookin', G. Once all of this shit pass, I'll be back chasin' a bag in the streets. You just make sure you watch your ass out here."

"Fuck you think I got this big mu'fucka for?" Chedda referred to the .9mm Kil-Tec in his lap. "And I got a vest on, just in case. 'Cause after niggas put my ass in this shit bag, I ain't takin' no chances."

"I feel you on that," Ace empathized. He knew how taking a bullet made a nigga cautious and quick to bust.

"Dawg, lemme get up outta here. I'll get with you whenever Paris decides to let your fool-ass come out and play," Chedda cracked.

Ace chuckled, and kiddingly replied, "Fuck you, Chedda."

Chedda push-started the Benz. As Ace was finna step out of the whip, his iPhone vibrated and he pulled it out of the pocket of his Chanel joggers, then checked its display. The incoming call was from Phat. Ace hadn't fucked with Phat since learning the nigga was on some police shit. For a while, he'd already been skeptical about Phat, but now he was sure of what type of nigga Phat is.

"Yo, be quiet. It's Phat callin'. Lemme see what he on real quick," Ace told Chedda. He answered the call on speakerphone. "S'up, Phat?"

56

"I'm just callin' to see if you wanna ride out to Chiraq with me and my boys later on tonight. I gotta go for a re-up. You down, or what?" Phat asked, utterly unaware he had been exposed.

Ace covered the mouthpiece on the phone, looked to Chedda, who was shaking his fuckin' head, and said, "This nigga got shit fucked up." Then in response to Phat, Ace spoke into the phone. "I ain't gon' be able to ride out with you tonight. Already got some other shit lined up." He played shit cool.

"That's cool. If you change your mind, then just hit me up and lemme know."

"A'ight." Without warning, Ace killed the call. He disgustingly spat, "That police-ass nigga think shit all good. Can't wait to blow him down!"

Chedda chuckled. "Chill, my nigga. We gon' down his ass."

"Fa sho."

Ace grabbed the bottle and took one more sip of the work. The two shook up once again before Ace stepped out of the Benz into the breezy evening air, and then Chedda dispelled down the street. As Ace walked into the crib, his phone vibrated and he saw there was a text from Savvy. With all of the drama in the air he hadn't really had time to talk with her much. He swiped the screen and read the message.

SAVVY:
Damn, longtime no see.

He wasn't trying to get caught texting back and forth with Savvy, so he glanced over into the kitchen to see if Paris was still busy. Once peeping that she was loading the dishwasher, he then texted Sav in reply.

ACE:
I'ma come see u soon.
Wassup tho?

SAVVY:

Just want u to know that I
went thru w/ the procedure.

He knew she was referring to having the abortion done. It was a relief because he understood that him having a baby with another bitch would more than likely be the end of his relationship with Paris. He texted her back.

ACE:
It was for the best of us
both. Keep yo head up.

SAVVY:
OK, Daddy. Luv u.

Ace left her last message on read. He then deleted the texts between them, just in case Paris decided to look through his phone again. Ace wouldn't stop fuckin' with Savvy because she knew her position. Although he would put Paris first because he really did want his family with her. Ace just wanted the best of both.

After loading the dishes into the dishwasher, Paris padded barefoot into the living room. She accidentally stepped on one of Adonis's toys, and cried out, "Ouch! Adonis, why do your ass have all of these damn toys out?"

"Take them toys into your room and play with 'em there," Ace directed his son.

"Okay, Daddy." Adonis began collecting his toys.

"C'mere, lemme rub your feet for you." Ace patted the seat beside him.

"Ace, please. I'ont want the cooties," Paris replied crudely. Knowing he would be checking out her ass in the fitted joggers she wore, she switched her hips hard as she ambled into their bedroom.

Ace trailed her into the bedroom and locked its door behind himself. "Paris, lately you been actin' so rude, and I ain't gon' lie, I miss the old you. I know I shouldn't have did what I did."

"Damn right, you shouldn't have."

"Just listen, bae."

"Then make it make sense."

He sat on edge of the bed, which she was lying in. "I know how bad I fucked up. But haven't a nigga always been here for you? All I'm askin' you to do is love me, even when it hurts. That's the only way we gon' get past this shit."

Tears slid down Paris's cheeks. "Ace, you hurt me so fuckin' bad," she wept.

"Bae, wipe your tears and stop that cryin'. I ain't mean to hurt you. Your ass mean so fuckin' much to me. You and my son. I love y'all."

"And I love you too. But don't take my love for granted," Paris warned.

"I won't." Ace used his hand to wipe away her tears. He leaned in, then kissed her lips and she didn't resist, encouraging him to kiss her with impetuous passion. Ace pulled his tank top off over his head and then helped Paris out of her closefitting T-shirt. Just as bad as he wanted to fuck, Paris wanted to fuck too.

Paris halted him. "Wait. What about Adonis?"

"Man, he in his room playin' with his toys, so we good," Ace said, easing her mind. He continued assisting her with removing the rest of her attire, then his own. Ace mounted Paris and she grabbed ahold of his erect dick and guided it within her moist pussy. A pleasurable moan escaped Paris's soft lips as Ace slowly slid back and forth in her. They both enjoyed the feel of each other's bodies.

Paris dug her manicured nails into the flesh of his back and groaned, "Yeesss, Ace. Yeeesss!"

"Damn, baby. I love how you say a nigga name," Ace whispered near her ear. He then commenced sucking on her earlobe and she liked the warmth of his breath on her neck. Ace drew back and peered into her eyes as he bit down on his lower lip, while beating the pussy up. He hooked one of her legs in the crook of his arm and dipped his hardness deeper in her snug slit with each thrust. The wetness of her kitty felt amazing to him! He leaned forward and sucked her hard nipples while he fucked her.

"Hmmm... Oooh, boy... It's so damn good!" Paris spread her legs wider in order to allow the tip of Ace's wood to hit her spot. She laid back with her head on the pillow and her back arched off the bed as the cum from her pussy creamed his dick. Pushing Ace onto his back, Paris climbed atop him, then planted her hands on his tattooed chest for support as she squatted her twat up to the tip of his thick pole and down onto its base. He watched with glee as his dick filled her hole. She spun around on the dick and began riding him reverse cowgirl.

"Bae, this pussy all a nigga need," Ace grunted. Gripping her hips, he matched her thrusts and she looked back over her shoulder into his eyes. She bounced and rocked on his pipe until it exploded. "Damn!"

Paris climbed off of Ace and laid in bed beside him. "Ace, don't think you can always fix everything with your dick, because I'm still a little mad at you," she said in a soft tone.

"Long as you still love me, then I can handle you bein' mad." Ace pecked her on the forehead.

"You know I love you like no one else could. If it isn't me, your sister, or your mama then a bitch shouldn't even show you no love. So, you better tell that other bitch to fall in line, because I don't play about mine."

Ace smirked. "Girl, I know you gang 'bout me and ain't playin' no games 'bout me."

"Period."

There was a small knock on the bedroom door, and they knew it was none other than their son, so the two hurried and pulled on their clothes. From the other side of the door, Adonis said, "Mommy, Daddy, me wanna come in."

"Okay, baby, here I come," Paris called out as she pulled on her T-shirt. She then opened the door and Adonis jetted by her straightaway to the bed and climbed in with his dad.

"Stop all of that jumpin' in the bed, boy," Ace told his son, who stopped jumping up and down immediately. He then gave Adonis his iPhone to play on.

Paris crawled into bed with both of her men, she just cared for their family to be happy. Ace lay with his girl at his side and his son in between them, he loved his family dearly. Paris and Ace wanted to be there for not only each other, but most importantly, Adonis. They couldn't let anyone tear their family apart.

Ace's phone vibrated and he grabbed it from his son then peeped that there was a video call from federal prison from his mother, Gale. It had been a week since he'd spoken with her last. He didn't like missing his mama's calls because he couldn't call her back. And he was looking forward to talking with her. Ace answered and Gale's smiling face showed on screen.

"Hey, son!" Gale greeted with excitement, seeing Ace.

"S'up, Ma?" Ace responded coolly. "Good to see you."

"Same here. Well, I'll be home next month, then we'll get to see each other in person."

"And I can't wait 'til then. Me and Mika gon' have a surprise for you on your first day out, and I'm sure you'll like it."

"What is it?" she wanted to know.

"Ma, you'll see for yourself. And don't even try to ask Mika, 'cause she ain't gon' tell you either," he forewarned.

Gale shook her head, laughing. "Good to know I ain't raise no snitches. Anyway, is that my grandson I hear in the background?"

"Yeah, his bad ass right here. So is Paris." Ace angled the camera so Gale could also see the others.

"Hello, Paris and Adonis." Gale waved at them.

"Hi, Gwanny! Me a good boy," Adonis chimed in.

"You better be," Gale told him.

Paris offered a wave of her fingers, then said, "Hey. I'll leave you two alone." She slid out of bed and headed into the adjacent bathroom.

Ace returned the camera onto himself. "She's just actin' all shy and shit."

"Paris seems like a real good woman for you. She takes good care of you and your son, and she's faithful. Boy, your ass better not lose that girl over some nothing-ass bitch."

"Evidently big sis told you about me gettin' caught creepin'." He was aware that like usual, Paris had called Mika and let her know about his sneaky link with Savvy, because his sister had turned around and called him to tell his ass just how stupid he could be at times.

"Sure did. And I'm not gonna say much to you about it, except you need to make sure you put your family first," Gale advised.

"I will, Ma," Ace assured, knowing his mama was right.

"So, how are you doing? And tell me the real."

He sat back up against the headboard. "Keepin' shit real with you, I wanna tell you I'm good with all of the money I'm up, but I still got some problems."

"Son, no amount of money can make all of your problems disappear, therefore you should enjoy it while you can. But always remember money comes and goes, so never let it make you. Because when it's gone, then you won't be shit without it," Gale philosophized. She just needed him to understand the good and bad of money.

"That's some of the realest shit I done heard, Ma," Ace praised. He realized money was most niggas' downfall in some way.

After spending time talking some more about things, there was only a minute remaining on the video call. Gale said her goodbyes to Ace, Paris, and Adonis before the call ended. Ace laid in bed beside his girl and son, with his moms on his mind. It felt good for him to talk with her, and some shit she had said resonated with him. He understood he had to make his family priority and never allow money to be what he lived and died for.

Chapter 8

It was night out and Ace n'em sat in the parked maroon Nissan Altima fiend rental, loading up artillery under the crescent moon. Ace occupied the back seat, making sure his Draco was ready for action. Chedda sat shotgun with the Kil-Tec in lap, and Sonny Boy was behind the steering wheel, his Glock .40 fitted with a drum lay atop the dashboard. Not to mention, Bookie, Poppa, and Sly all poled up in the tinted-out Tahoe SUV that was parked some down the street. They were awaiting Phat to pull up, with his rat ass.

Phat was under the impression he was coming to meet up with Sonny in order to serve him ten bricks, but he wasn't expecting for Ace and Chedda to be present. After learning Phat was the rat who snitched on Baller, Ace n'em had plotted to pull a back door move on him. The ten bricks would just be a consolation after killing Phat, it would be a win-win. Sonny had given him a remote location to meet with him, and Phat agreed. Unbeknownst to Phat, he was about to fall into a rat trap.

"Fuck is this fat ass nigga at?" Ace asked no one in particular. He was just eager to get the job done.

"Nigga texted me he's on the way 'bout ten minutes ago," Sonny Boy said as he checked his Rolly for the time.

"Sure he didn't see what's up, so he's not comin'?" Chedda thought.

Sonny snorted. "His ass is too damn blinded by money to even see all money ain't good money. I'm sure he'll pull up soon."

"So, Sonny, what whassup with Blue talkin' savage shit on social media?" Ace wanted to know. He'd recently seen another video on *Facebook* of Blue talking murder talk.

"Fuck dude," Sonny replied bitterly. "When I ran into him at our moms' crib, I let him know he'll have to buy back Forty's chain if he really want it. He had the fuckin' heart to up pole on me right in front of my mom, talkin' 'bout I better make you run him the chain, or else. If it wasn't for Moms makin' him put the pole away, I'ont know what that nigga would've done. But I do

63

know this, he got me fucked up if he think I'ma let some shit like that slide."

"I'ont do that internet beefin', that type of shit is for bitch-niggas. So, if Blue keep on comin' outta his mouth, then I'ma send somethin' around his way," Ace threatened.

"It is what it is."

Chedda peeped through the rearview mirror as headlights of a vehicle approached from behind. "Look, here comes Phat weak-ass now."

Ace grabbed his Drac', and said, "It's go time. I'm sure bro n'em ready. Sonny, you just play shit cool, and we'll do our part."

"Fa sho," Sonny Boy replied as he grabbed his .40 from the dashboard.

Ace and Chedda hunched down in their seats so Phat n'em wouldn't be able to spot them inside the sedan, being that Phat was expecting to meet with Sonny alone. The silver Benz G-550 Wagon pulled curbside, parking in between a rock and a hard place, having Ace n'em occupying the sedan in back and Sly n'em occupying the SUV in front. Before stepping out of the sedan, Sonny pocketed his pole, he then made his way to the back door of the G-Wagon and climbed into its back seat beside Phat. He couldn't help but notice Phat, along with Nice and Troy, each with their guns out, so Sonny felt comfortable placing the Glock in his lap while he and Phat talked money.

Discreetly, Ace and Chedda slipped out of the Honda with their weapons in hand then began creeping towards the G-Wagon. As planned, Sly pulled up in front of the G-Wagon, with the Tahoe's blinding high beam headlights on. Then Bookie and Poppa jumped out of the SUV with their guns ready for action. Instantly, Nice and Troy pushed opened their doors, hurried out the front seats of the truck and opened fire.

Blocka, blocka, blocka, blocka!

Rrraa, rrraa!

While Nice and Troy engaged in a pop out with Bookie and Poppa, they weren't aware of Ace and Chedda creeping up on them from behind until it was too late. Ace and Chedda filled their backs with slugs, causing Nice and Troy to crumple onto the ground. Then Ace and Chedda pulled open the back doors on either side, finding Sonny Boy holding Phat at gunpoint. Once the Tahoe had pulled up, Sonny upped his ratchet on Phat and confiscated his. He slapped Phat across the face with the ratchet and split his brow, before pointing the barrel at his top and demanding him not to move. Phat never expected for Sonny Boy to pull a back door move on him with Ace n'em.

Leaving Phat to Ace and Chedda, Sonny grabbed the duffel bag filled with ten blocks as he stepped out of the G-Wagon. He noticed Nice on the ground still fighting for his breath and weakly reaching for his choppa beside him, so Sonny Boy popped Nice twice more in the head before returning to the fiend rental.

"Bitch, thought you was gon' just get away with snitchin' on Baller?" Ace hissed as he pressed the Draco's barrel to Phat's chubby check.

"M-man, it ain't even like th-that," Phat stuttered, holding his hands up.

"It's straight like that. We seen the paperwork, and the only reason the feds ain't came to get you yet is 'cause you workin' with 'em," Chedda piped in.

"Listen, p-please don't kill me," Phat begged for his pathetic life. "I'll do anything, just—"

Boc, boc, boc, boc, boc!

Not caring to hear shit else out of his mouth, Ace knocked Phat's shit back with shots to the head. Phat's heavy corpse slumped to the side, with half of its head missing, while blood and brain matter was left splattered about the expensive interior of the G-Wagon. Ace and Chedda hurried to the fiend rental then skirted away from the scene with the others in the Tahoe trailing. They left the air filled with gun smoke.

Martell "Troublesome" Bolden

Chapter 9

As Ace pushed his Infiniti through traffic on his way to the hood, he listened to Tee Grizzley's track, "Locked Up." He had Paris riding in the passenger seat and Adonis was strapped into a seatbelt in the back. *Can't believe the day has finally come for my ma to come home after all these years*, Ace thought.

Today, Gale was finally coming home from fed prison, and Ace was looking forward to it. Aside from some video calls, he hadn't seen his mom in the past six years she had spent locked up. And now that Gale was coming home, Ace wanted to be there for her on her first day out, he just wished his lil brother, Glen, could be there too. He knew their mom wasn't always there for them due to her past lifestyle, but at least she always loved them.

Ace had a surprise for his mom and was sure she would love it. While Mika went to pick up Gale from the Greyhound bus station Ace decided he would meet up with them at the house in the hood. Ace knew the feeling of getting out of prison, so he wanted his mom to feel at home.

"Ace, I noticed you've been kinda quiet all morning. Ain't you excited to see your mom?" Paris asked. She understood he'd had a strained relationship with Gale over the years. He had told her some about it, but Paris knew they were growing close ever since Gee's death.

"Yeah, I am. It's just that I wish Gee could be here too." Ace sighed.

Paris reached over and rubbed his back in comfort. "Baby, I'm sorry your little brother can't be here with y'all. Just remember he's the reason you even decided to give your mom a second chance."

"You right. Good lookin' for comfortin' me, boo." Ace braked at a stoplight. "I know once my ma meet you, she gon' love you," he assured.

"I can't wait to finally meet her in person. More importantly, I really want her to meet her grandson, with his bad ass." Paris looked into the back at Adonis, who was pulling loose his tied

67

shoestring on his Air Jordan's 9's. "Little boy, leave your shoestrings alone. You ready to see your granny?"

"Yep! Where my gwanny at?" Adonis said excitedly.

"We on the way to her house now. And your lil ass best not be actin' bad around your granny," Ace forewarned his son.

On the way, Ace made a stop at Walmart so Paris could pick up some party favors. While she and Adonis were inside the store, Ace remained outside, where he stood leaned back against the car as he *FaceTimed* Mika.

"Hey, bro. What's up?" Mika answered. Ace could tell by her background that she was in the bus station. He asked, "Where's Mama?"

"I'm still waiting on her. But her bus should arrive in the next ten minutes. Don't worry, bro, she'll be home soon."

"Damn, big sis, I can't believe she finna come home after all these years. I know for a long time I was heated at her for not bein' there for us and shit, but now I just to want her to be in my son's life."

"Trust me, lil bro, Mama knows how much she missed out on being in me, you, and Glen's lives. We just gotta give her a chance to be here now."

"I feel you. But it ain't gon' be the same with Gee gone now," Ace uttered.

"One thing for sure, he may be gone but he'll never be forgotten," Mika expressed. "Ace, you just make sure to be at the house when we get there. And where's Paris and Adonis?"

"They're in the store pickin' up some shit for the homecomin' party. And don't trip, I'ma be at the crib fa sho." He looked over and saw Paris and their son exiting Walmart, she was carrying a bag in one hand while holding Adonis's hand in her other. "Look sis, I'm finna jump in traffic. I'll see you at the crib in a minute."

"Okay, see you soon. Love you, bro."

"Love, sis." Ace ended the call and then pulled the passenger door open for Paris, who handed him the bag before entering the car. Then Ace sat Adonis in the back seat alongside the bag before he made his way back behind the wheel. He dipped back into traffic on the way to the hood.

Once arriving at the house, Ace parked curbside. Paris stepped out and also grabbed Adonis and the bag from the backseat. Before stepping out himself, Ace reached beneath his seat and grabbed his switch, then placed it on his waistline. While Paris went inside to set up the party favors, Ace remained outside sitting on the front porch steps with his son. He waved at Reverend Johnson, who was watering his front lawn.

Ace observed the hood, he couldn't believe this was where he had lived his entire life. The goal was to get out of the hood without forgetting where he was from. But shit, part of Ace didn't even want to leave the hood. Although he understood it was what was best for him, if he didn't want to fall victim to the plague of gun violence associated with young hood niggas, like his little bro, Gee.

Ace's eyes landed on Gee's shrine filled with memorabilia near the tree right in front of the house. Damn, he missed his lil bro. And he wished Gee could be there right now to see their mom also. After Gee's unfortunate death, Ace realized how one could be here today and gone tomorrow. It's not that Ace was afraid of dying, he just cared to live for his girl and their son.

Paris stepped out onto the porch. "Ace, everything is all set. And the décor looks nice in there, I'm sure your mom will love it," she commented.

"Good. 'Cause I just really want her to feel at home. She deserves to live in a place where she can be comfortable, not some damn cramped cell," Ace replied, reflecting on his time spent locked up.

"Listen," Paris began as she took a seat beside him on the steps with Adonis in between them. "I know you're anxious about seeing her after it's been so long. Just make sure you tell her how you feel."

Ace pondered that a moment. "Paris, I got mixed feelings. Regardless, she's my moms, and I'ma respect that."

Soon thereafter, Mika pulled up and parked her Mitsubishi Eclipse Cross SUV across the street. Once Mika, Breon and Gale exited from the vehicle, Ace stood and descended down the steps to go and embrace his mom. She looked the same as he last seen her, the only difference was her hair was in long dreadlocks and she put on a little weight.

Gale was brown-skinned, shorter, with a big ass and large titties that she rarely displayed, due to wearing male attire to fit her tomboy persona. She had always been tomboyish, but now she fully embraced it and was even a dyke. Ace could respect that Gale had no shame in her lifestyle.

"Hey, son!" Gale cried out excitedly as she approached Ace, who she noticed had grown up so much. "Damn, you're a grown-ass man now, I see."

"Yeah, Ma, I am. Shit, it's like I went from a baby to man," Ace told her.

"I know, but you're still my baby. Now, give your mama a hug, son." Once Gale and Ace embraced, she squeezed him tightly and felt the bulge of his Glock. Gale leaned back and looked into his eyes, then said, "Boy, what're you doing with that big-ass gun?"

"Ma, this ain't even my biggest one." Ace smirked. "Anyway, it's good you home. Now you can meet your grandson." He turned to his son and called out, "C'mere, Adonis and meet your granny."

Paris carried Adonis down the steps, then placed him on the ground and he ran over to Ace and Gale. Seeing her grandson caused Gale to smile widely as she thought about how Adonis favored Ace so much at that age. She scooped Adonis up in her arms.

"Oh, my goodness, you look just like your daddy!" Gale gushed. "You happy to see Granny, Adonis?"

"Yeah!" Adonis exclaimed. "Me wanna stay at you house."

"Okay, you can stay at my house with me." Gale noticed the very pretty girl standing there. "And this must be Paris."

Ace wrapped an arm around Paris's waist and introduced them. "Yeah, this her. And bae, this my ma, Gale."

"Hey, nice to finally meet you," Paris said shyly.

"Girl, you don't gotta be all shy and shit with me. Ace told me all about you, it's like I know you already."

"All good things, I hope. Well, welcome home."

"Thanks, girl." Gale placed Adonis on the ground, and he ran off to play with Breon.

Paris decided to step away as Mika approached her mom and brother. It was obvious to Paris that they needed some time alone as family. She took Adonis and Breon inside the house for some snacks.

"It feels so good for me to be here with y'all right now," Gale commented. "But of course, it also hurts that Glen isn't here with us."

"He's here in spirit, Ma," Mika said.

"That's why we keep his shrine here," Ace added.

Gale grew misty-eyed at the sight of Gee's shrine. She couldn't help but to think about all of the time she had missed out on in her kids' lives, and now sadly Gale wouldn't be able to spend time with Glen at all. She understood she couldn't make up for the loss time, so she would just have to enjoy the time that they have together.

"Listen Ma," Ace began gingerly, observing Gale grow emotional. "Lil bro knows how much you wish he was here. Just know that Gee loved you, no matter what."

"Yeah Ma, Ace is right. We all love you no matter what," Mika input.

"That means a lot to me, because I need the love of my kids," Gale expressed.

"We got you, Ma." Ace pecked Gale's forehead.

Gale noticed Reverend Johnson on his front porch, who she had known since she was merely a child. She offered him a wave, which he returned along with a smile. Rev prayed Gale would make her late mother proud and do right from now on.

There was a blue Volkswagen sedan that came speeding up the street that caused Ace to clutch the butt of his Glock. The Volkswagen sped on down the street and Ace was relieved he didn't have to put in some gunwork right then and there. But Gale had peeped how patient he was but ready to bust. And she understood it was just the way shit was in the streets, although she didn't want for the street life to claim both of her sons.

"Ma, let's step inside the crib real quick, 'cause me and Mika got somethin' to show you," said Ace.

"What is it?" Gale inquired.

Mika led her by the hand towards the house, and responded, "Just come on, Ma, so you can see for yourself."

Once they entered the home Gale came upon a renovated and refurnished placed. The exterior of the house had even been painted with a fresh coat of white. After Mika had moved out, she and Ace decided to renovate and fully furnish the entire house for their mom. They just wanted Gale to feel at home, especially Ace, because he knew how it felt to come home after doing time on lockdown in a cell. And Gale thought the place was beautiful, it was exactly what she needed to welcome her home.

"We thought you needed a nice home to call your own, considering where you just came from," Mika said.

"Plus, we couldn't just let Grandma's crib be abandoned. So, we fixed it up just for you," Ace piped in.

"This is real nice what y'all did for me. Your grandma left us this house, so I appreciate that it means as much to y'all as it does to me," Gale expressed.

"I got one more thing for you, Ma. Follow me," Ace told her. While Mika stayed back, he led Gale through the lavish house, then out the backdoor and there parked in the backyard was a brand-new, pearl white Lexus NX350 SUV. "That's yours, Ma."

"That is so damn nice, son!" Gale squealed as she checked out the whip.

"Told you I got you once you came home, Ma. And here's some cheese to hold you over." Ace dug out a bankroll worth twenty G's and handed it to her.

She turned to Ace and met his eyes, then humbly said, "Ace, I can't thank you enough for not only all of what you're doing for me, but also for being willing to give me another chance at being in your life."

"Keepin' shit real with you, at first, I was only willin' to just so you can have a bond with my son. But then I realized that I need a bond with you too. Right before Glen was killed, I had convinced him that he and I should give you another chance, and I'm keepin' my word to him."

Gale could tell just how much love Ace had love for Glen. "Son, it's good to know you love your little brother to death. Now, you gotta live for him. While taking care of everybody else, sometimes you can forget yourself. Just make sure you do your all to watch yourself in the streets."

"Ma, in the streets, I'm movin' right by dodgin' opps and twelve. I ain't lettin' shit stop me from gettin' rich. Plus, I keep a pole on me, in case I gotta get on some savage shit," Ace assured.

"Don't be so sure of yourself when it comes to these streets, Ace. You know I ended up getting indicted due to someone else talking, and your dad ended up getting murdered because of lacking. All I'm saying is, these streets don't have love for anyone," Gale forewarned.

Ace had to admit his mom was right. "Listen Ma, one thing I learned in the streets is a nigga can be betrayed by love."

"Son," Gale planted a palm on his cheek, "that's why we need people in our life that love us unconditionally."

One thing for certain, Ace understood love could get him killed if he underestimated it.

Martell "Troublesome" Bolden

Chapter 10

Arriving at the crib, Ace pulled into the driveway and parked beside Paris's whip. After being out for most of the day catchin' plays with Chedda, Ace wanted to drop off some money, so he wouldn't have as much on him at once. One thing for sure, Ace didn't want to be a walking lick.

Once Ace and Chedda stepped out of the car, they made their way inside the house. Upon entering, Ace found Adonis in the front room, seated on the floor before the huge flat screen TV playing *Call of Duty* on Xbox.

"Hey, Daddy and Uncle Chedda!" Adonis exclaimed.

"S'up, lil nigga," Ace said and rubbed his son's peanut head.

Chedda sat on the floor beside Adonis and grabbed the second joystick. "Lemme play the game with you and show your lil ass how to do this shit."

"Me gon' shoot you ass!" Adonis blurted out, causing them to chuckle.

"Adonis, language!" Paris scolded him as she emerged from the hallway, which led to the master bedroom.

"It's cool, bae. He's just kickin' it with the guys," Ace said.

"No, it's not cool. That's why his ass is so damn bad now, because y'all be influencing him so much."

"Ace, your girl's right, my nigga," Chedda piped in, siding with Paris.

"Thank you, Chedda," Paris responded. "By the way, how is Antoinette and the girls?"

"They're all good. You know I make sure home is taken care of."

"As you should, unlike some niggas," Paris sniped, her anger still evident. She went into the kitchen.

Ace sucked his teeth. "Dawg, I can't believe you took her side like that."

"Whatever, nigga," Chedda chuckled. "Go ahead and do what you came to do so we can bounce."

Turning for the bedroom, Ace went to put away the money he had made. He put the bankroll in the top drawer of his bedside nightstand. Afterwards, he made his way into the kitchen, where Paris was prepping dinner.

"Damn, bae, it smells good in here. What you cookin'?" Ace asked Paris as he wrapped his arms around her waist from behind.

"Lasagna and garlic bread. I'm sure you'll like it," Paris said.

"You know how I like to eat. Listen, bae, I'll be back later."

"Just make sure you're back for dinner."

"I will," he assured.

Paris looked over her shoulder at him and added, "And you better not leave me and your son waiting."

Ace pecked her cheek before walking into the front room. He told his son he'd be back and then Ace and Chedda bounced. Outside, the two returned to Ace's Infiniti.

"What you wanna get into?" Ace asked.

"Let's go to the hood and meet up with the gang," Chedda told him.

"A'ight." Ace drove away from the curb.

While they slid through traffic, Babyface Ray's tune, "If You Know, You Know" played in the background. Chedda hit up the pill man named Mane along the way, so he and Ace could cop some ecstasy. Ace made a detour to meet up with Mane at a liquor store. Chedda placed the glizzy on his waist before stepping out of the foreign. Ace remained in the whip as Chedda went to Mane's silver Lexus and got in. After dealing with the pill man, then Chedda headed into the L-store as the Lexus went on its way. A few minutes later, Chedda returned to the whip with two bottles of orange juice for them to sip on while they jig off the pills. Ace and Chedda jumped back in traffic.

Ace's phone chimed, he grabbed it and noticed there was a *FaceTime* call from Savvy. Once he answered, he could hear the loud music blaring in the background of the club and overheard Savvy cursing out someone.

"Fuck goin' on?" Ace wanted to know. She didn't hear him due to her heatedly yelling profanities. "Sav? Talk to me."

Finally, Savvy appeared on screen, she appeared to be wet and was very angry. "Dude, tell me why this fuck-nigga just got mad at me 'cause I wouldn't give his ass a lap dance, so he threw a drink on me!" she raved.

Hearing the shit that took place had Ace heated, because there was no way he would let any nigga treat his bitch like that. "Who's the nigga?"

"Toucan's soft ass," she reported. "He got me fucked up, 'cause I ain't one of his lil dusty hoes that he can treat any way he wants."

"That nigga still there?"

"Yep, he still sitting in VIP, like he can't be touched or some shit. And he cappin' like he ain't worried about you."

"A'ight. Me and Chedda on the way." Ace redirected the whip and headed towards the club Sav worked, putting the pedal to the metal. "You good, Savvy?"

"Yeah, I'm okay. The fucked-up part is when the owner of the club heard what had happened, his ass came at me like I'm the one in the wrong, just because Toucan's bum-ass hoes make the club a little money."

"Check it out, leave that club right now. Matter fact, it's your last night even workin' in that piece of shit. I'ma deal with that nigga Toucan, once we get there," Ace declared.

"Ace, don't do too much."

"Bitch, just do as I say and leave right now. I know what I'm doin'," he told her firmly.

"I am finna leave. I'm just grabbing my shit out of the dressing room real quick." While she was in the dressing room, Nina hurried in. Savvy told Nina they needed to leave ASAP, then Nina started to pack up her belongings also.

"Y'all asses best be gone by the time we get there," Ace warned. "I'll see you at your crib later." He ended the call without warning.

Chedda chased down an X-pill with some orange juice, then said, "What's the move?"

"Finna pull up to the club my lil bitch work at and check the shit outta this nigga for sneak dissin'. That's the same clown-ass nigga I was tellin' you about named Toucan, who pimps on a few hoes I was tryin' to get in our club. Apparently, the nigga salty 'cause his ass can't have Sav."

"If the nigga so pimpin', why he actin' like such a peon?" Chedda shook his damn head.

"I'ont know. But I'm finna pimp-slap the shit outta his ho-ass when I catch him," Ace stated. He downed an X-pill with a sip of his juice.

During the drive, Savvy texted Ace in order to let him know she and Nina had left the club. He and Chedda soon arrived at the club, then Ace drove by to see if he could spot Toucan's car. The chameleon-painted Cadillac CTS sittin' on chrome rims was parked across the street from the club's entrance. Ace busted a U-turn in the middle of the street and parked two cars behind the 'Lac. He checked his Rolly and noticed it was still early in the night, therefore Ace knew Toucan wouldn't be coming out soon, so he could check the nigga for sneak dissin' on him. He realized Toucan figured he would barge into the club making a scene, but Toucan was in for a surprise.

Ace wanted Toucan to understand it wasn't necessarily about a bitch, but it was more so about the fact he was disrespecting Ace by treatin' his bitch like shit. Ace wasn't the type of nigga to beef over a bitch, because he always put money over bitches. However, he understood his bitch was a reflection of him, so he had to stand up for her.

Close to half an hour came and went when Ace peeped Toucan step out of the club surrounded by three of his hoes. Ace grabbed the Glock and stepped out of the foreign as Toucan n'em were crossing the street. With the gun in hand at his side, muzzle facing the ground, Ace hastily approached Toucan. Once Toucan peeped Ace there, he forcefully pushed one of the screaming girls into Ace, hoping it would give him time to jump into his 'Lac to get away. Ace shoved the girl out of his way onto the pavement as he went after Toucan, and once he caught up with the nigga trying to jump into the driver side of his 'Lac, Ace slapped him across the face with the blick.

Boc!

"Argh, shit!" Toucan yelped. Once Ace struck him with the gun, the firearm accidentally discharged. Luckily for Toucan, the bullet just barely missed his head and only his left ear ringing. Plus, Toucan was bleeding badly from the laceration left on his forehead, which he had suffered from the strike of the gun.

Patrons who were awaiting to enter the club scattered every which way once the shot rang out. The club's security guards kept their distance, not wanting to engage in a possible shootout. Chedda had slid out of the whip and was perched up on its hood with his stick out on full display in his hand while watching Ace's back, he was patient but was ready to squeeze.

"Stupid-ass nigga, see, you almost made me smoke you on accident," Ace snarled. He pressed Toucan back up against the 'Lac and stuck the barrel of the Glock to Toucan's eye socket as he patted him down but found no pistol. Afterwards, Ace took a step back and held the blick facing downward at his side. "Now, listen up, nigga. I ain't really trippin' over you throwin' a drink on Sav, but what you ain't gon' do is keep sneak dissin' on me, like I'm one of those niggas that'll let you slide. I'ont know what you'll do for your respect, but I'll die for mine."

"A'ight! I'll pay you respect! I just don't want no beef with you. I'll even let my hoes come work in your club, if that's what you want. Bruh, just please don't shoot me," Toucan pled.

Ace liked making the nigga cop a plea in front of his hoes, so the girls could see what type of nigga they were really fuckin' with. He stuffed his switch in the pocket of his Amiri jeans. "I'ont want your hoes workin' in my club now. And I'ont want you to pay me respect, instead, you can pay me in cash. So, if you don't want no smoke with a nigga, then you gonna have to cash me out. I'ma need fifty G's come Friday. I'll meet up with you by Savvy's crib around midnight to collect. If you don't show up, or you try to pull some stupid shit, then I'ma light your ass up like my Rolly bezel," he asserted.

"I'ma show up, and you don't have to worry about me tryin' to pull some shit on you. That's on my life," Toucan swore, scared to death.

"Then I hope you wanna keep your life," Ace forewarned. As he turned and headed back towards the Infiniti, he overheard Toucan shouting at his hoes.

"Y'all hoes hurry the fuck up and get y'all punk-asses in the 'Lac!" Toucan shouted.

"You wasn't just talkin' tough like that to the dude with the gun," one of the hoes had the nerve to comment.

Toucan spun on the heels of his Tom Ford loafers then pimp-slapped the hoe. "Listen here and listen clear hoe, don't you ever again talk back to pimpin'!"

Ace just shook his head as he slid back behind the steering wheel, and Chedda returned to the passenger side. After push-starting the whip, Ace skirted away from the curb down the street with the engine blurring.

"Dawg, you had that coochie nigga scared as fuck," Chedda chuckled.

"His ass lucky I didn't blow his mu'fuckin' head off. He gon' have to run me fifty bands, or I'ma have lil bro n'em spin on him," Ace stated.

"What about Savvy?"

"I'ma go check on her and see if she's good. She and Nina ain't workin' in that club no more, we just gon' have them work in ours as bartenders."

"That's cool. Speakin' of, we have plenty of bitches set to show up and audition for Baddies on Saturday. Then our club will be open for business in a couple weeks from now," Chedda told him.

"That's whassup. And we gon' make sure that bitch lit!" Ace responded. He merged into the turning lane.

"Facts. Bro, listen, drop me off in the hood real quick then you can go and check on your side-bitch. Just don't get caught up by wifey again, player," he half-joked.

Ace committed his turn and laughed. "Players fuck up too." Subsequent to dropping off Chedda, Ace headed to Savvy's place. He parked behind the house and then made his way to the back door. Using his key, Ace entered then went into the front room, where he came upon Savvy and Nina seated on the couch, smoking a blunt of exotic weed and looking at somethin' on Nina's iPhone. Both appeared to have taken showers, since Sav had her hair wrapped in a towel and Nina's long hair was still partially wet. Not to mention, they wore robes.

"Whassup with y'all?" Ace said as he stepped over and sat betwixt the girls.

"Hey, Ace. Boy, you a fool!" Nina exclaimed.

"Hell you talkin' 'bout, Nina?" he inquired.

Savvy handed him the phone so he could see for himself. "Ace, I told you not to do too much. Obviously, somebody filmed the shit you did to Toucan, because it's posted all over social media." She puffed the weed.

Ace saw himself on video treatin' Toucan. He wasn't aware the incident was being recorded, and he really didn't even give a fuck. Handing her back the phone, he commented, "That's what dude lame-ass gets for talkin' so much shit. And he gon' have to cash me out, or else. I ain't playin' games with no niggas in these streets."

"Period," Nina input. "Lots of niggas need to get fucked up for being bogus, just like Phat." Like many people, she had heard via social media that Phat got smoked for being a snitch, and part of her believed Ace had something to do with it.

"Phat got what he had comin'," Ace replied neutrally. He changed the subject. "As for that club, don't worry about even workin' in that bitch no longer. Me and Chedda gon' have Baddies open before this month over, and y'all can work there."

"Good. 'Cause a bitch gotta secure the bag," Sav said.

"Ain't that the truth?" Nina added.

Ace grabbed the blunt and took a pull of the strong weed. "I respect y'all are all about a bag. That's what makes a bitch bad. Most bitches think just 'cause of their looks they're bad, it takes for her to be a hustla with confidence to be considered a bad bitch." He was aware Savvy and Nina marketed their assets in order to get paid, and he didn't judge them for it.

"Ace, that's what makes you so one-hundred, you don't judge a bitch for what she do, or be on some jealous-ass shit, instead you respect her grind," Sav complimented him.

"And you better believe there isn't many niggas like you," Nina chimed in.

"Big facts," he agreed, then hit the weed.

Savvy couldn't get enough of how fine Ace was to her, with his brown skin and deep waves. Just his vibe and drip turned her on, plus she was attracted to how savage he was. Sav couldn't help herself, so she straddled Ace's lap and seductively kissed him. He palmed her phat ass in his free hand. She grabbed the back of Nina's head and pulled her in for a three-way kiss. The trio shared lips and tongues with each other, and all of them were enveloped in the moment.

Nina rose to her feet, then dropped her robe and exposed her naked body, she sat back beside the others on the couch. Ace helped Savvy out of her robe, leaving her nude while on his lap. Nina lay back on the couch with her legs spread and using her fingers to play with her pierced pussy, and the others enjoyed the show as Nina set free soft moans while sliding her fingers back and forth in her twat. Savvy climbed in between Nina's agape legs and began licking and sucking her clit, causing Nina to moan aloud. Ace stood and pulled his joggers down around his Air Jordan's, he then positioned himself behind Sav and guided his hard dick into her gushy honeypot.

"Damn, this pussy slippery," Ace mentioned as he fucked Savvy from the back while she feasted on Nina's twat. He slapped Sav's ass as he slid his large piece balls deep into the pussy, all while he locked eyes with Nina.

"Mmmm... Eat this pussy, girl," Nina moaned. She pushed Savvy's mouth onto her kat as she came, and Savvy lapped up Nina's fluids. Knowing that she brought Nina to orgasm made Savvy's pussy so hot and wet on Ace's dick as he dug her out.

Savvy played in Nina's pussy with her fingers while she took every inch of Ace's hardness deep in her slit, and she loved how he fucked her rough. "Oooh, shit, Ace! Yessss... Fuck me like that," she cried out as she reached climax. "That's it, baby! Yessss!"

Nina climbed onto her feet and kissed Ace while he continued smashin' Sav. Once Ace pulled his dick out of Savvy, Nina pushed him back onto the couch and straddled him, she slid her wet-shot down onto his wood then bounced on his lap. Sav sat beside Ace and kissed him passionately while he caressed her titties. He took turns kissing Savvy and sucking Nina's titties as she rode him. The pussy felt so damn good to Ace.

"Aw shit, I'm finna bust a nut!" Ace groaned, feeling his dick tingle. Nina climbed off his lap then she and Sav knelt before him, both girls shared the pleasure of sucking his big dick. While Savvy held the base of the dick, Nina worked her warm mouth on its tip. Joining in, Sav sucked his balls. Ace leaned back in his seat and puffed the weed while he watched the girls give him sloppy-toppy at the same damn time. He pulled Nina's head back by her hair as his dick exploded and semen slid down its base. Both girls lapped up his sperm at the same time as their tongues interacted, and they kissed each other while Ace watched the girl-on-girl action.

Following the threesome, the girls sat on the couch on either side of Ace, both still naked. He couldn't stay with them for the rest of the night because he had already assured Paris he'd be back home in time for dinner. After Ace had been caught by Paris fuckin' with Sav on the side, he didn't want to go through that shit again. He knew it wasn't right that he was still fuckin' with Savvy, although it didn't mean he loved Paris any less. And Savvy just played her position.

Ace took himself a quick shower before leaving the girls to themselves as he headed home. During the ride, he texted Paris he was on the way. Thinking about the dinner Paris had prepared, Ace realized that more than anything, he was hungry for money.

Martell "Troublesome" Bolden

Chapter 11

Tonight, auditions were being held at Baddies, and there were numerous bad bitches of all kinds in attendance. After ads had been posted on social media, more girls showed up to audition than expected. The strip club was lavishly decorated, from the main stage to the VIP lounge to the champagne rooms. All that was missing were the strippers.

While Ace and Chedda sat in front of the main stage, they watched as girl after girl took to the stage to dance for them. Thus far they had hired several girls on the spot. Not to mention, Savvy and Nina already had their spots secured, both as bartenders. The next baddie took to the stage, she was brown-skinned with tattoos on her chest and thigh, her hair styled in long blonde butterfly-locks, piercings in between her cleavage, and a body only Dr. Miami could give. She wore a red coochie-cutter cat suit with red patent leather, knee-high stilettos.

"Introduce yourself," Chedda said.

"I go by Toy, I'm twenty-two years old, and I flew out here from Texas," Toy told them in her southern drawl.

"Spin for us, so we can see what you workin' with," Ace requested. Toy did a seductive twirl, giving them a good look at her assets. "That's whassup. Now, go ahead and work the stage."

Once the music was cued, Toy began putting on a sexy performance. She slow wound her hips and seductively licked her lips. Then she made each ass cheek bounce separately, before twirling around the pole and ending by landing into the splits. Toy knew how to put on a good show for sure, just what the club needed.

"Shorty, we 'preciate your time, and your audition was fire," Chedda told her. He turned to Ace. "What you think?"

"All of these bitches bad!" Ace exclaimed.

"I know, but we only need about twenty of 'em. So, we gotta narrow it down."

"What if we just make sure we pick all different flavors of bitches, that way our club will have somethin' for every nigga to choose on."

85

"Good idea. 'Cause we both know niggas will cash out on what they like."

"Fa sho," Ace concurred. He sipped from the bottle of Rémy then looked to Toy. "You hired, boo."

"Good thing we posted ads on our social medias since that mark-ass nigga, Toucan, didn't wanna let his tired-ass hos work here," Chedda commented. "By the way, what ever happened with that situation involvin' dawg?"

Ace smirked. "Dawg sweet ass ran me that fifty racks, 'cause he don't want no smoke. His ass lucky I didn't Debo him for more than that."

"Type shit." Chedda knew how his nigga was, and he wanted to see Ace living by boss standards instead of living by the gun. "Listen Ace, we done bossed up. So now we gotta live that shit. A lot of the shit that we used to do, it's not for us no more. That's what we got niggas around us for. I ain't sayin' put your gun down, I'm just sayin' put it up until it's really needed. Feel me?" he expressed.

"Yeah, I feel you, my nigga."

Chedda shifted towards him. "And now that we about to get the club up and runnin', I'm not gon' be in the game for much longer. It's time to go legit. After we move the next load we cop, then I'm outta the game for good."

"Bro, I respect your decision to go legit. But I also respect the game. So, you do you, and I'ma do me."

"Just keep in mind that the game ain't fair," Chedda warranted. "Anyway, we're s'pose to meet up with Shane in a couple days, so have your portion of the re-up money ready."

"Been ready," Ace assured. He sipped from the bottle of Rémy.

"No doubt. Now, let's get back to these auditions."

"Let's do that."

As the night went on and more girls auditioned, Ace and Chedda chose the ones they wanted to work for them at Baddies. Now that they had their roster of girls for the club, a grand opening was the next move.

Subsequent to the auditions, Ace and Chedda parted ways. Pulling up at Savvy's crib, Ace parked the Infiniti and then went inside. By the time he got there, Sav was in bed asleep, so he tried not to wake her as he got into bed with her. He spooned her while they slept.

The next morning, it was early in the am as Ace was in the front room seated on the couch recounting his portion of the re-up money on the coffee table, which was supposed to amount to a hundred-and-twenty-five racks. Savvy sat beside him, rolling up a blunt of cookie weed. The TV was on with muted rap music videos showing.

"Ace, what's all of this money for?" Savvy inquired as she sprinkled buds of weed inside of a Backwoods blunt.

"It takes money to make money. Stop always askin' about my business," Ace told her and sat a stack of money onto the pile.

"Anyway, I was thinking about being a video vixen."

"What made you think about some shit like that?" Ace wanted to know.

"'Cause a casting agent seen me on *OnlyFans* then slid in my DM, saying he think I have what it takes. And guess what, he wanna fly me out to ATL, so I can audition for a spot to be in a music video with Lil Baby."

"That's whassup, boo. When you s'pose to be flyin' out there?"

"This weekend. That's when I have to be there to audition." Savvy sparked up the blunt and took a puff.

"I know you gonna slay it," Ace assured. "Speakin' of auditions and shit, we finally picked all of the girls to dance at Baddies. And instead of bein' on stage, you and Nina gon' bartend."

"That's cool with me, 'cause I'ont really like niggas lusting over me anyway. So, when is the grand opening?" She hit the blunt once more before passing it to Ace.

"That'll be in two weeks. And we gon' make sure it's litty," Ace told her. He hit the blunt, filling his lungs with thick weed smoke. "Now, help me count up this paper real quick, so I can make sure it's ready."

While the two sat side by side, hand counting the money, there was a knock at the front door. Ace figured it must be Nina coming over so damn early as Savvy went to answer the door. After pulling open the door she found her brother, Dre. Savvy stepped aside and allowed him inside. Once Dre stepped in the front room then he peeped Ace there with all of the paper piled up on the coffee table. Dre's eyes grew big in size because he had never seen that much money at once before, but he also noticed the Glock on the side table in arms' reach of Ace.

When Ace looked up from counting a stack of money and saw Dre standing there, Ace instantly felt some type of way. Savvy couldn't help but peep how the two mean-mugged one another. Now that Dre had witnessed Ace there playin' with so much money, Ace had it in mind to remove his stash from Savvy's crib ASAP because frankly, he just didn't trust the nigga.

"What're you doing here so early, Dre?" Sav asked, trying to cut the tension.

"Damn, a nigga can't drop by to check on his sis or some shit," Dre remarked.

"Boy, you know your butt is welcomed here. But what are you really doing here?"

"Need to holla at you alone, sis." Dre cut his eyes at Ace.

Beggin'-ass nigga probably need some cash, Ace mused bitterly. But he kept that thought to himself. Instead, he said, "Sav, I'll be in the bedroom." He then grabbed the pistol and stepped away with it in hand, leaving Savvy and Dre alone to talk about whatever as he headed into the bedroom. While Savvy talked with her brother, Ace went into the closet, where his stash was. He grabbed a Nike gym bag, then began placing all of his cash, product, and artillery inside of it. Ace wouldn't take a chance leaving his shit there, so he would just have to stash it elsewhere. And he knew exactly where that would be.

Savvy entered the room, and said, "My lil brother's gone now." She noticed him packing up his things. "Ace, what're you doing?"

"I'm finna take my shit somewhere else," he told her as he put his Draco in the bag.

"But, why?"

"I can't have my shit here with your lil bro all in my business now. 'Cause I'ont trust lil dawg like that."

"Dude, Dre won't do no shiesty-ass shit like that, so stop trippin'," she tried convincing him.

Ace eyed her, and replied, "Sav, money make mu'fuckas do shit they wouldn't normally do all of the time. I just ain't willin' to take no chances." He grabbed up the bag and then returned to the front room, with Savvy on his heels. He started tossing all of the bread from the coffee table into the bag.

Savvy stood with her weight shifted to one side and her arms crossed. "Ace, just make sure you remember I'm here for you."

"Sav, it's not like I'm done fuckin' with you, boo. I'm just finna stash this shit somewhere else, just in case."

After Ace finished putting the rest of the money in the bag, he headed out the back door since his whip was parked behind the house. He tossed the gym bag onto the back seat and then slid behind the wheel. Once Ace jumped into traffic, he was on his way to his home with Paris, where he would stash his shit. There he would protect his family, his home, and his stash with his life.

Martell "Troublesome" Bolden

Chapter 12

It was evening when Ace stepped out of his house. He made his way to Chedda's Benz-Jeep, which was idling in the middle of the street. Once Ace hopped into the passenger seat then Chedda pulled off. They were on their way to see the plug, Shane.

"Put your half of the re-up money in that tote bag, along with mine," Chedda instructed.

Ace grabbed the tote bag off the back seat, then placed his half of the money inside. "Where we meetin' up with Shane?" he asked.

"Final Detail carwash. Then we'll take the work to the trap spot and bust it down."

"A'ight, cool. I need to holla at Sly anyway."

"'Bout what?"

"Some bread he owes me for a front," Ace let him know. "You know the rule."

"Yeah, if you ever get fronted, spite whatever, always pay that money," Chedda pointed out.

Arriving at the carwash, Chedda pulled the Benz-Jeep into the lot and parked beside Shane's Aston Martin DB9 that was being detailed. Shane was dripped in a Burberry 'fit and bust-down Patek timepiece, with a FN handgun on his waist. While Shane entered the back seat of the Jeep, his two boys stood posted outside on security.

"Whassup, homeboys?" Shane greeted the two.

"We good," Chedda replied.

"We'll be better once we get them bricks," Ace added.

Shane took off the Burberry backpack filled with twelve kilos of coke then passed it to Ace. "Those bricks are uncut."

"Good." Ace peeped inside of the backpack to check out the bricks for himself. Once satisfied with the product, he then handed Shane a tote bag filled with a quarter-mil in cash money. "It's all there."

"No doubt." Shane took a look inside of the bag and saw the paper-cheese. He knew that Chedda and Ace always came with their money right, so he didn't even bother to count it up. "Just hit me up whenever y'all ready to re-up."

Chedda looked back at Shane and said, "Listen, after this load, we won't need to do any further business. With the strip club and shit, there isn't a need to stay in the game. Feel me?"

"Yeah, I feel you," Shane replied.

"Speak for yourself, Chedda. I'ont need nobody to help me get paid," Ace chimed in. He didn't peep how Chedda eyed him. "Shane, I'll handle business with you while Chedda handle business with the strip club."

"Sounds good to me," Shane said. "Speakin' of y'all strip club, make sure I get an invite to the grand openin'."

"Fa sho," Chedda assured. "We'll be in touch."

Shane dapped the two before stepping out of the Jeep with the tote bag in hand. Chedda pulled out of the carwash lot into traffic while Ace kept his eyes peeled for Twelve. During the ride to the hood, Ace noticed that Chedda was unusually quiet. He figured that Chedda had some shit on his mind. But what?

Once they made it to the hood, Chedda pulled to the curb in front of the trap spot. He stepped out the vehicle and Ace grabbed the backpack, then followed suit. They made their way into the spot and found Bookie, Poppa, and Sly there in the front room shooting dice.

"Come and get in this gamble, so I can take y'all paper too," Poppa suggested as he shook up the dice inside his closed fist.

"Nigga, just roll the damn dice," Bookie insisted. He wanted to win back the money he had lost thus far.

Chedda walked through the middle of their gamble disregardful, and stated, "We don't got time for that shit right now 'cause we got business to take care of." He went into the kitchen.

Sly looked to Ace and inquired, "Fuck wrong with him?"

"I'ont know," Ace responded, thrown by Chedda's attitude. "I'ma go and see whassup." He followed Chedda into the kitchen and sat the backpack on the table. "What's on your mind, Chedda?" Ace peeped that his boy seemed bothered.

"Ace, lemme holla at you one-on-one real quick," Chedda requested.

"A'ight." Ace trailed Chedda outside onto the front porch, where they were alone. "So, what's good, brody?"

Chedda leaned back against the banister. "Listen, my nigga, that shit you said to Shane about you don't need nobody wasn't cool. How the fuck can you say some shit like that when we need each other just the same."

"Chedda, all I was sayin' is I'ma do me just like you gon' do you. If you wanna leave the game and go legit, then I won't try to convince you otherwise. But I'ma go hard in the mu'fuckin' paint 'til the death of me."

"Bruh, you really need to listen to the shit that you're sayin' right now." Chedda shook his damn head. "If your ass was smart then you'd be tryin' to get outta the game too."

Ace cocked his lip. "Dawg, there's a lot of smart niggas in a cell too."

"Just like there's a lot of hard niggas in a casket," Chedda remarked. He stood erect. "Nigga, if your ass gonna be stupid enough to keep playin' around in this game, then that's on you."

"How're you heated at me for wantin' to stay in the game, just 'cause your ass on some soft shit and wanna get out. You trippin'."

"'Cause I give a fuck about what happens to you. And miss me with that soft shit, Ace. I ain't none of the niggas you be treatin'."

"Fuck you mean by that? Huh, Chedda?"

"I mean, those niggas scared of you enough to let you treat 'em however you feel, but I ain't goin' for none of that shit."

Ace scoffed. "Bro, just fall back before... Never mind." He reconsidered the remark he was finna make because, due to his love for Chedda, he didn't care to say something that he couldn't take back.

"Before what, nigga?" Chedda pressed as he stepped into Ace's personal space. He felt like what Ace needed from him in that moment was some tough love.

"Get the fuck outta my face, Chedda. On Gee, I ain't playin' with your ass right now."

"Do it look to you like I'm playin'? Like I said, I ain't none of the niggas you be treatin' like hoes."

"Yeah, whatever," Ace replied cavalierly.

As Ace started for the front door of the trap, he thrust shoulders with Chedda, which caused Chedda to forcefully push Ace in the chest and make him stumble backwards. After Ace found his balance, he then stormed Chedda and the two engaged in a tussle. Once Bookie, Poppa, and Sly overheard the tussling on the front porch, they all hurried outside and got in between Ace and Chedda, before things could turn into a fistfight. Ace and Chedda were still trying to get at each other while being held back, their boys had never seen the two so heated at one another.

"You two niggas need to chill the fuck out," Bookie told them both while restraining Ace.

Poppa, who was blocking Chedda, stated, "Y'all better than this."

"Hell goin' on between y'all niggas any fuckin' way?" Sly probed from the sideline.

"Dude soft ass heated 'cause I'm doin' me and shit," Ace accused.

"Nah, nigga, I'm heated 'cause you always doin' some stupid-ass shit," Chedda retorted. He calmed himself, remembering Ace is his mud brother. "This nigga actin' like I'm tellin' his ass somethin' wrong about changin' up the game. Ace, we in this shit together, so no matter what we decide to do on our own, it's all love."

Ace's temper lowered. "So, you do whatever you feel's best, and I'ma do my thang. But one thing we ain't gon' do is show fake love," he sniped.

"Fake love? Ain't shit fake about me, nigga!" Chedda barked. "You know what? I'ma get up outta here. Just put that work up for now." He descended down the porch steps and headed towards his whip. Bookie went after him as Chedda slid behind the steering wheel. Once Bookie approached, Chedda rolled down the passenger window.

"Damn, big bro, you just gon' leave us like that?" Bookie said.

"Man, I can't be around that nigga Ace, right now."

"Want me to ride with you?"

"Nah, I'm good, lil bro. I need to go and clear my head, that's all," Chedda let him know as he push-started the whip.

"A'ight, I feel you. Just hit me up later on." Bookie shook up with him before Chedda smashed away from the curb and went on his way. Once Bookie returned to the porch he looked to Ace, and said, "Fam said he just need to go and clear his head. You need to fix shit with him, 'cause y'all beefin' isn't what any of us need."

Ace snorted. "Whatever. Chedda's just in his chest right now. Anyway, fuck that shit. Sly, drop me off real quick."

Sly chirped the alarm on his Jag truck as he and Ace headed for it. Once they were inside, Sly dispelled down the street on the way to take Ace to his destination. Arriving at a stop sign, Sly braked on the corner of 6th and Burleigh Street.

"You a'ight?" Sly asked as he lowered the volume on the stereo.

"Shit, I'd be better if you go ahead and light up the rest of that blunt in the ashtray," Ace suggested, needing to get high right now.

Sly grabbed the remains of the blunt, lowered the window a bit, then tossed the blunt out. "That was some bullshit weed, and I know you don't smoke that. I need some of that smoke you keep on deck."

"Good thing I got a few grams of za on me."

"It should be some blunts in the middle console."

Ace searched the middle console and found a Backwoods blunt. "After that shit with Chedda back at the trap spot, a nigga need to get blowed bad as a bitch." He began splitting the cigar down its center with his thumbnail.

"Dawg, Chedda just wanna see you do more than move work," Sly said in Chedda's defense.

"And ain't shit wrong with that, but Chedda gotta understand I'm movin' work to feed my family. So, I need all the cash I can count up," Ace laid out as he dumped the tobacco from the cigar into the ashtray. "Speakin' of, when you plan on cashin' me for that brick I fronted?"

Sly hesitated, then replied, "Don't trip, I got you soon." He changed the subject, "Where do you want me to take you to?"

"Take me to my side bitch Savvy crib," Ace answered. He told Sly the location.

"A'ight. But first, I'ma need to stop for some gas 'cause the tank damn near on E."

"Stop at the G station, I'll give you gas money." Ace filled the blunt with buds of exotic weed and then rolled up the Backwoods.

Once the light flipped green, Sly pulled off with traffic. During the ride, Ace and Sly passed the blunt back and forth. Sly made a stop at a gas station, and while he went inside to pay for the petrol with the money Ace had given him, Ace remained in the whip with the stick in his lap, closely watching out for any opps. After Sly pumped the gas, he returned inside the whip and jumped back into traffic. Arriving at the destination, Sly veered to the curb across the street from the house Ace had pointed out, where his Infiniti sat parked in front.

"Good lookin' on the ride," Ace said.

"No problem," Sly replied. "Listen, think I can come in and use the bathroom, 'cause I gotta take a piss like a mu'fucka?"

"Yeah, c'mon."

As Ace departed from the whip, so did Sly. Leading the way, Ace entered the house with Sly in tow. They came upon Savvy in the front room, seated with her feet folded beneath her on the couch while talking into her iPhone on *FaceTime* with Nina. She couldn't help but notice Ace was accompanied by the same nigga she had gotten a funny vibe from the last time she'd seen Sly. Ace gave Sav a peck on the lips, then directed Sly to where he would find the bathroom and Sly beelined there.

While Sly was using the bathroom, Ace went into the kitchen in order to tame his munchies from the weed, he grabbed himself a big bag of Doritos chips from the top of the fridge. As he returned to the front room, Sly emerged from the bathroom.

"A'ight, my nigga, I'ma get up with you later," Sly said.

"Fa sho." Ace showed Sly to the front door and let him out. Once he turned around, he then found Savvy leering at him. "Fuck is your problem?" He dug inside the bag of chips and ate a handful.

"Nina, lemme call you back, girl," Sav told her homegirl before ending the call. She gave Ace her undivided attention. "Why the fuck did you bring dude to my house? I done told you I got a funny feeling about him, Ace. Ugh, your ass just don't listen."

"Sav, I'ont wanna hear shit about none of my niggas right now. I already bumped heads with Chedda a lil while ago over some bullshit."

"I don't see how, 'cause Chedda is a good nigga. What happened with you and him?" Savvy was sympathetic because she thought Chedda was a real friend, unlike Sly.

Ace placed his Glock on the end table, then took a seat on the couch beside her. "Didn't I just tell your ass I'ont wanna talk about none of my niggas? Besides, I'll deal with that shit on my own. You just stay in your place."

Savvy smacked her lips, jumped up to her feet, and stormed off into the bedroom then slammed its door shut. It was apparent to Ace he had managed to piss her off, although he didn't mean to. He just wasn't the type of nigga to pillow talk with any bitch concerning drama with his bros. But it wasn't like Ace didn't take heed to what Savvy thought, he understood she believed Chedda was a real one, but he didn't understand why she had an opposing perspective towards Sly. Maybe her woman's intuition was more telling than his male ego.

Ace did want to get some pussy from Sav in order to ease his mind, but he knew she wouldn't let him fuck her tonight as upset as she was. So, he grabbed his iPhone then logged onto the *PornHub* website and watched an erotic film, until he had fallen asleep on the couch. One thing for sure, he didn't sleep on no beef.

Chapter 13

Pulling the Infiniti curbside, Ace parked in front of Gale's house. He was there to check in on his mom. Since she had come home, Ace tried spending as much time with her as he could. In doing so, he realized Gale had a lot of game to offer him, based upon her experience in the game before. Ace had grown closer to his mama, he just wished Gee was there to share in that.

Pushing open the driver's door of the whip, Ace stepped out into the season-shifting weather and put the switch on his waist. He peeped Reverend Johnson on his porch observing him. Ace waved at Rev as he headed towards Gale's front door. When he stepped inside, Gale was in the front room sitting on the couch with a pretty redbone bitch in her lap. Ace was aware that his mama was now a lesbian, and that was her prerogative.

"S'up, Ma. See you enjoyin' company," Ace said.

"Yeah. This is my girlfriend, Yolanda," Gale introduced, and Yolanda offered him a wave of the fingers. She nudged Yolanda out of her lap, who now sat beside her. Gale lit up a Newport, then asked, "What brings you by?"

Ace took a seat on the couch across from them. "Just wanted to check in on you real quick."

"Well, I'm doing good so far, thanks to you and Mika making sure I don't need for nothing. However, I'm still trying to get back used to being free."

"I know how that feels. Just take your time, Ma. One thing for sure, I'ont want you gettin' back in the game," Ace told her.

Gale puffed the cigarette. "And what about you, Ace? Maybe you need to leave the game alone too," she suggested.

"Man, now you soundin' like Chedda. Since we got the club, now he wants to fall back from the game and go legit. That's cool and all, but I just need a lil more money before I can decide to do that."

"Take it from me, if you keep telling yourself that, then no matter how much money you make, it will never be enough. This is why you gotta be smart with your money and invest it in legit avenues. So, it sounds to me that Chedda is telling you the smart thing to do. And I advise you to take heed."

"Maybe you right." Ace didn't dispute Chedda was doing the smart thing by deciding to get out of the game before it was too late, he himself just wasn't quite ready yet. He understood what came with the game, most of the real ones more than likely either ended up in a cell or a casket. And changing the game was the best way to avoid those outcomes.

"Anyway, why didn't you bring my grandson by with you?" Gale asked.

"'Cause he's out with Paris. I'll be sure to bring Adonis with me next time," Ace assured.

"I like Paris a lot, she's a good girl for you. And I can tell how much you love her. She deserves you to be there for her.

"Ma, me and Paris gon' be a'ight, 'cause no matter what I do in the streets, I'ma always take care of home."

"Just don't let her lose you to the streets, like I did your dad," she reminded.

"That's why I watch my rear view at all times," he let her know. "Look, I'm finna bounce. You need some cash, or anything?"

"No, I don't need nothing at all."

"A'ight. Take care, Ma."

Before leaving out, Ace offered Gale a hug and promised to bring Adonis by soon. Outside, he walked towards the Infiniti and slid behind the steering wheel. He drove around the corner, then pulled up at the trap spot. Bookie, Poppa, and Kiki were chillin' in Kiki's newly purchased sleek black Subaru VRT sedan parked across the street. Lately, Kiki could be found hanging out with the gang and was gettin' her money and weight up with them. And they all liked having her around in the spirit of Gee.

Ace exited his car and then made his way into the back seat of the Subaru beside Bookie, who had his pistol in his lap. He said, "What's the deal?"

"We just came from taking Kiki to stand on a nigga about some bread that he owed her," Bookie replied.

"Yeah, the nigga thought shit was sweet 'cause she a bitch," Poppa piped in. He was in the passenger seat.

"A bad bitch. Get it right," Kiki input from the driver's seat.

"So, what happened?" Ace wanted to know.

"I pistol whipped that nigga and made him pay up what he owed," Kiki told him.

Pop laughed at the thought of how the shit had gone down. "Big bro, Kiki a savage, just like Gee!"

"Kiki, don't ever let a nigga play you outta no paper," Ace gamed her. "Speakin' of, where the fuck that nigga, Sly, at?"

"We ain't seen his ass in about a week now," Bookie informed.

"That nigga owe me some paper too. I been hittin' him up but he hasn't answered. If y'all see him before me, let his fool-ass know to holla at me ASAP," Ace laid out.

"We got you," Kiki responded.

"Anyways, whassup with you and Chedda though?" Poppa asked.

Ace sucked his teeth, then said, "I ain't talk to dawg since me and him bumped heads."

"Fam, it's been almost a week since then. Y'all niggas need to let that shit go," Bookie suggested.

"Don't trip. I'ma holla at Chedda and straighten shit out. That's my bro, and I love his lil soft ass." Ace chuckled.

Kiki chimed in, "And you know Glen wouldn't like seeing his two big bros against each other, because it's supposed to be y'all against all odds."

"That's real," Ace replied. This made him think more about Chedda's decision, Ace knew he and his bro needed to rap. Raindrops began spattering on the Subaru's windshield. The clouds were gray as the season was inching towards fall. Ace still wanted to fuck the city up with one more stunt before the summer was completely over with. And he would grind all winter with the hopes of stacking more than enough paper to take the whole next summer off.

"Listen, I'm finna slide. I'll catch up with y'all later," Ace told them. He departed the whip and pulled the hood of his Palm Angel hoodie up over his head as he jogged through the rain to his Infiniti. Inside the whip, he grabbed his iPhone, then sent Chedda a text.

ACE:
Bro, text me yo Addy.
We need to talk.

A moment later, Chedda texted in reply. It was the first the two interacted since bumping heads.

CHEDDA: I'm at our club. Pull up.

ACE: OTW.

Ace wasn't surprised Chedda was at the club making sure everything was just right, being that the grand opening was coming up. He push-started the foreign and then pulled away from the curb. During the commute to the club, Ace was listening to Fredo Bang's tune, "Top." His mind was all over the place. Thoughts of all the shit he and Chedda had been through and all the niggas they had tended to swam through his mind. It had been nearly a week that the two hadn't spoken to one another since the night they bumped heads, and after much deliberation, Ace knew it was only right to straighten shit out with his boy.

Soon thereafter, Ace pulled up to Baddies and parked curbside behind Chedda's Benz-Jeep. He departed the Infiniti and then made his way into the club. He found Chedda standing behind the bar, doing inventory on the bottles of liquor.

"S'up, my boy. Still heated at me?" Ace grinned and took a seat on one of the barstools.

"I ain't even thinkin' about your ass right now, 'cause I've been too damn busy tryin' to make sure the club ready to open," Chedda replied casually.

"Listen, Chedda, I know this club venture mean a lot to you, especially since you wanna get outta the game and go legit. One of the main reasons why I even invested in this shit with you is because I support what you're on. Trust me, I understand that us goin' legit is what's best, and one day I'll make that decision. But for now, I still wanna run' it up in the game."

"Even though I don't agree with you, Ace, I can't do shit but respect your decision. You know how the game goes, so make sure you play for keeps."

"Fa sho," Ace assured. "And my bad for that fake love comment. I know you're too real to be on that type of shit."

"Dawg, you bet not ever come at me with no shit like that again. You lucky lil bro n'em was there to get me off your ass, or I woulda fucked you up!" Chedda half-joked with a smile.

Ace chuckled. "Nah, my nigga, you the one who's lucky lil bro n'em was there, 'cause your ass can't fuck with me. But on some real nigga shit, you know I got love for you, bro."

"And I got nothin' but love for you too, no matter how much your fool-ass be doin' the most. You my bro for life."

They had been like brothers since jumping off the porch as lil niggas, and both of them always had different ambitions, Ace wanted to run the game while Chedda wanted to change the game, although they both respected how each other played the game. After all the wins and losses they endured together, there wasn't much which could cause the mud brothers to fall out.

Ace took a gander around the establishment, admiring its interior design. "Can't believe this bitch is finally finna open soon. And you made this shit happen, my boy."

"Fam, we made this shit happen together. Now all we gotta do is stay free and alive," Chedda expressed. He gathered two glasses and sat them atop the bar, then grabbed a bottle of Rémy off the top shelf and poured them each a drink. "Let's drink to this."

"Let's."

The two grabbed up the drinks and clinked their glasses, then took a swig of the liquor. After all of their time and money invested in the club, it was due to open in just a few days. Chedda would use the establishment to go legit, while Ace would utilize it to launder illegitimate gains. They both had come up from the bottom and wasn't trying to go out while on the top.

Chapter 14

Stepping out of the Infiniti, Ace made his way into Paris's boutique, her newly open cute little spot located downtown. The establishment was called At Your Best, and offered women's apparel, hair products, cosmetics and sex toys. It was a proud thing for Ace to have helped his girl open up her place of business, and thus far business was good.

Inside, Ace came upon a store filled with all female shoppers and saw Paris servicing one of them. Once she noticed him there, Paris waved over one of her employees to deal with the customer.

"Hey, baby," Paris greeted Ace as she approached him.

"Hey to you, too," Ace replied. "I see business is steady pickin' up."

"Yes, it is. And I love being able to help other women feel like bad bitches."

"Well, not one of these bitches in here badder than you."

Paris blushed. "Boy, will you stop. Any who, what brings you by?"

"Just thought I'd check in on you. See if you need me for anything," Ace told her.

"Well, I do need for you to pick up your son from daycare in an hour. Because as you can see, I'm swamped with customers, and I don't think I'll have time."

"Say no more. Anything else?"

"Um..." She thought about it briefly. "Also, it'll be nice if you grab us something for dinner, preferably Chinese takeout."

"Damn, you want me to clean the house too?" he joked.

Paris playfully pushed him. "Boy, whatevs!" she laughed. "I'll see you at home around nine o'clock tonight. Lemme get back to my customers."

The couple pecked lips, then Ace turned for the door and left Paris to tend to her customers. Once outside, Ace returned to his whip parked near the curb out front. brought the engine to life, and then when he saw the coast was clear through his mirrors, he gunned away from the curb down the street.

Subsequent to scooping up his son from daycare, Ace pulled up in front of Gale's crib and parked. He saw Gale was seated on the front porch steps, along with Yolanda. Once Ace and Adonis got out of the car, Adonis ran over to his granny with Ace following. Gale grabbed up Adonis and wrapped him in her arms.

"Hey, Gwanny! Me had fun today at daycare," Adonis said.

"That's good," Gale replied, then smooched him on the cheek. "Boy, you look more and more like your daddy every time I see you."

"That's exactly why he's so damn handsome," Ace chimed in jokingly.

Gale laughed. "Let's just hope he doesn't end up being so damn cocky like you. At least he gets his good behavior from Paris."

"Trust me, Ma, that lil nigga bad as hell. I stay havin' to whoop his ass for some shit."

"He's not bad, he's just adventurous. You and your brother used to be the same way at his age," Gale pointed out.

"I remember back in the day, when I was like five or six and Gee was about two, he saw me jump out the lower window, so he did it too and hurt himself. Then Mika told on us to you, and you whooped my ass bad," Ace reminisced, able to laugh about what had happened back in the day.

"Mm-hm, I remember when that happened. I just wish I would've been there for all of my kids more, then I'm sure things would be much different for y'all. All we can do now is move forward."

"Ma, don't worry about it. Now you have the chance to be here for our kids and make a difference in their lives."

"And I will."

The pearl white Beamer made its way down the block and pulled curbside, then parked across the street from Gale's place. Mika and Breon stepped out of her boyfriend's whip, while Money Mel remained inside behind the steering wheel enjoying the air conditioning. Out of his respect Mel offered a wave to Gale and she waved back. Also, Mel acknowledged Ace with a nod of the head and Ace returned it. Mika and Breon approached the family, Gale gave Breon a hug, and then he and Adonis set off to play.

"Hey, everybody. What y'all talking about?" Mika asked.

"We were just reminiscing about how bad your brothers were back in the days. Breon and Adonis remind me of them every time I see them together," Gale responded.

"Right," Mika agreed.

"Damn, sis, I see you lookin' all good and shit," Ace complimented her. She had her hair and nails done up and was wearing a cute Fendi outfit with some diamonds around her neck.

"Mel keeps me and my son looking good. In fact, he bought this outfit from Paris's boutique."

"So, shit serious with you and Mel? I see you made y'all relationship official on the *'Gram*," Ace pointed out. He actually thought the nigga was better for her than others she fucked with in the past.

"Yeah. He treats me and Breon how a real nigga is supposed to. I like being with him," she answered.

"Girl, just continue to make him work for some cookie," Gale advised her.

"Of course, Ma. This cookie is not free."

Ace shook his head. "I'ont wanna hear that type of shit." The girls all laughed at him.

"Maybe I need to tell Paris the same," Gale replied.

"Look, I'ma go holla at Mel while y'all talk about girl stuff." Ace made his way across the street to the passenger side of the BMW and slid in. Per usual, he peeped that the nigga was drownin' in water around his neck and wrists. The two dapped.

"What's to it?" Mel opened up.

"Ain't nothin' to it but to do it."

"Indeed." Mel shifted towards him and said, "Heard about what happened to that police-ass nigga, Phat."

"Somebody had to do it to him," Ace responded coolly.

"And Baller says he wants to reward whoever did the hit."

"No need. That shit was outta love, loyalty, and respect for the big homie. Next time you get the chance, give Baller my number and tell him to hit me up."

"I got you."

"No doubt. Check it out, the grand opening of our club will be on Friday. And I want you to be sure to show up in support. Post it up on your social medias 'cause we want all the ballin' niggas and bad bitches in the Mil there that night," Ace told him.

"You got it. Just make sure I'm VIP," Money Mel requested.

"Cool. Long as my big sista don't mind you bein' there."

"Homeboy, I respect your sis too much to even play with her emotions like that. Plus, she's a real bitch, and a nigga ain't gon' find that in many bitches nowadays. But Mika ain't gon' have shit to worry about anyway, 'cause I'ma bring her there with me," he expounded.

"Good thing sis finally bagged her a real nigga," Ace input. "I'm finna bounce. I'll get with you soon."

"Before you go. You got some of that good smoke on deck?"

"Always." Ace pulled out his sack and tried to give Mel seven grams on the love, but Mel insisted he wanted to support his hustle and paid up. They dapped once again before Ace stepped out of the whip.

Ace said his parting words to Gale n'em before he collected his son and headed for the Infiniti. He opened the driver's door and put his son in the car, then made him climb into the back seat. Ace pulled off down the street and drove on his way.

After making a stop to pick up some Chinese takeout, Ace and his son was on the way to the crib to Paris. By this time night was falling, so he flicked on the headlights. During the commute, Ace texted Paris that they were on the way with the food, and she replied she couldn't wait to see them.

Seeing that he needed some gas, Ace steered the whip towards a gas station. He soon arrived at the G station, where he pulled into the lot and idled his vehicle with a foot on the brake at an available gas pump. Ace saw some niggas standing in front of the station, then grabbed his pole from his trap compartment and sat it in his lap. As he was finna put the car in park, suddenly a red Mazda 6 with tinted out windows braked to a hard stop beside him. Ace peeped what was up a little too late, as a nigga jumped out of the passenger side and now held him at gunpoint.

"Bitch-ass nigga, if you try somethin', I'ma pop the shit outta you," the hooded figure barked as he reached through the rolled down driver's window of the Infiniti and grabbed the pistol out of Ace's lap.

Once the gunman leaned into the window, Ace noticed the nigga was actually Sonny Boy's brotha, Blue. In that moment, he knew Blue had come to collect the chain of his dead homeboy, Forty. And also, his life. When Ace had laid down Forty for Sonny Boy, along with some bricks and cash, Ace had taken Forty's bust-down Cuban link chain from his neck before leaving him for dead.

Blue ravaged through Ace's pockets, taking all of his money. "Now take the fuckin' chain off and gimme back my nigga's shit!"

"A'ight, you got it." Ace complied, not wanting to give Blue any further reason to smoke him in front of his son. He removed the chain then tossed it at Blue's feet as a diversion and skirted off.

Blocka, blocka, blocka!

Bullets from Blue's switch rapidly struck Ace's whip, leaving several bullet holes in its rear window and trunk as Ace fishtailed out of the lot. Ace weaved through vehicles, just barely avoiding an accident in order to get away. Glancing over his shoulder into the backseat at a wailing Adonis, he was relieved to see his son wasn't physically harmed. Ace heatedly slammed a closed fist down onto the steering wheel. He wasn't heated over the possessions taken from him, instead he was heated at the fact Blue had put his and his son's lives in grave danger. And now Ace was thirsty to shoot Blue to death.

Ace grabbed his iPhone and immediately called up Sonny Boy. He just wanted to let his nigga know not to get caught in the crossfire.

"What it do?" Sonny answered.

"Blue just stripped me and tried to burn me while I'm with my son!" Ace reported heatedly.

"What?"

"Dawg, I know you said you'll handle him 'cause he's your bro, but I told you if he brings beef my way, then I ain't never been the type of nigga to call off no beef. And the fact that he pulled that shit while I'm with my son is the reason why I'ma really drop his ass."

"Listen, you my nigga and he my brotha, but loyalty makes mu'fuckas family. And real talk, Ace, you been more loyal to me than Blue. You already know his ass upped stick on me in front of our moms. So, fuck dude hoe-ass. Do whatever you gotta do, my nigga," Sonny encouraged.

"Trust me, I am. I just wanted to let you know how I'm comin' so you don't be in the way," Ace told him. Following the phone call, Ace was ready to slide on the pussy-ass nigga, Blue.

Arriving at home, Ace circled the block thrice before feeling safe enough to park the car in the back driveway beside the Honda Accord. He stepped out of the car, holding Adonis in one arm and the bag of takeout in his other hand. Examining the bullet holes left in the Infiniti, he noticed one of the bullets had struck just several inches from where his son was sitting in the back seat. The shit made Ace so fuckin' mad to see it, and he couldn't wait to get down on Blue whenever that time came.

"Listen, son, we ain't gon' tell your mama about what happened, 'cause we don't want her to be scared. A'ight?" Ace told his son.

"Alwight, Daddy. Us don't wanna scare Mommy," Adonis said in his bravest tone.

"Good." Ace knew how Paris would overreact if she heard about his and Adonis's lives being put in danger, and Ace just didn't care to worry her.

Ace and his son made their way into the back door of the crib. They found Paris in the front room seated on the couch, and Adonis ran over to her. Ace sat the bag of food on the coffee table, then took a seat beside his girl and gave her a peck on the lips. He was as happy as Adonis to see her. Ace realized that for the sake of his family, he needed to do his all to protect them from his street affairs.

Martell "Troublesome" Bolden

Chapter 15

Needing to get away from the street life for at least a couple of days, Ace had decided to take his girl and son on a road trip to the Wisconsin Dells Water Park. With all that was going on in the streets, he wanted to spend some time with his family, away from all of the bullshit and take some time to unwind. Being that they would be staying over the weekend, Ace had booked them a suite in the water park's five-star hotel. He just needed to be able to relax without being worried about the possibility of him being caught slippin' by opps or twelve. So, for now, Ace wanted to enjoy time away with his girl and son.

While Ace was sliding down one of the waterslides with Adonis, Paris was seated poolside, looking all cute in her black and gold Chanel one-piece bathing suit and wearing oversized Chanel sunshades. Her hair and nails were freshly done. She loved seeing Ace interact with their son. More than anything, Paris cared for them to be a happy family. With how Ace was living, she was afraid she could end up losing him and be left to raise their son on her own. So, Paris cherished every moment she was afforded the opportunity to be with her man and son together.

Ace treaded through the waist-deep water while holding Adonis in an attempt to teach him to swim. He let go of Adonis, who kicked his tiny legs and floated, due to the floaties he wore. They swam over to the edge of the pool where Paris was. Ace grabbed Adonis and lifted him out of the pool, Adonis ran up to Paris, while Ace remained in the water near the poolside.

"Mommy, come swim with me and Daddy," Adonis said.

"Uhn-uhn, Mommy just wanna sit here and relax, baby," Paris told him.

"Please, Mommy!"

"Maybe later, okay?"

Ace splashed some of the water on Paris, and said, "Girl, come get your ass in this water with us right now."

"Ace, will you stop, before you get my hair wet?" Paris cried out. Like most Black women, she didn't play about her damn hair.

"You ain't your hair. Now come take a swim." Ace splashed her once again, causing his son to giggle.

"Again, Daddy, again!" Adonis exclaimed, and Ace obliged by splashing her rapidly and soaking her hair and all.

Paris hurried to her feet and laughed. "Now look at what you did to my hair. Ugh, you play too much!" She ran and jumped in the pool, playfully going after Ace. He grabbed her and dunked her underwater, while Adonis excitedly watched from poolside. Once Paris resurfaced, she and Ace splashed water all over each other, having a water fight. Paris grabbed Adonis then pulled him into the water with them, and the trio played in the pool together.

Afterwards, Ace, Paris and Adonis went to grab a bite to eat. They sat at an outside table near one of the many eateries the water park had to offer. Their food was delivered, and they all enjoyed cheeseburgers and curly fries, with different flavored milkshakes. Paris picked the onions off Adonis's burger because he didn't like them and gave them to Ace. She didn't mind catering to both of her boys.

"You and your son are always making a mess," Paris commented, seeing both had drops of ketchup on their shirts.

"Like father, like son," Ace replied with a mouthful of food.

"He definitely have your ways. Sometimes I don't know if that's a good thing or a bad thing, that he's so much like you. I'm just glad he's a mama's boy."

Ace thought about it a moment. "Good thing he is a mama's boy." He took the final bite of his burger and then looked down at his son, who picked up a curly fry from his lap and stuffed it into his mouth.

"Ace?"

"Yeah?"

Paris studied him, and said, "Are you ever gonna propose to me?"

Ace wiped his mouth with a napkin. "Thought we already agreed on this, Paris."

"Correction, *you* agreed on us being good without a ring on my finger. But the truth is, I would love for you to commit to me, unless you don't care to be with me."

"Who's been fillin' your head with this shit? Nett? You know I wanna be with your ass, so stop trippin'."

"Nett don't have nothing to do with this. It's just at times I can't help but get the feeling you won't commit to me, because you're too damn busy creepin' on me with some bitch. Especially the nights when you don't come home to me and your son."

"Paris, where all of this shit comin' from? You don't gotta worry, 'cause I ain't fuckin' with that bitch Savvy like that," Ace deceived. He knew Paris was still suspicious of him stepping out on her after catching him with Savvy.

"And if I find out you are, I'ma fuck you and that bitch up," she forewarned. "What I can't understand is why are you always running the damn streets, while me and your son are at home."

"Man, I just be in the streets chasin' a bag, that's it."

Paris shook her head. "Might as well be cheating on me with the streets, as much as you spend time in them. Ace, I want to be your wife, not just your main bitch."

"Listen, you are a nigga's wifey. A ring won't make a damn difference. Long as I make sure you and my son good, then it shouldn't be a problem. Didn't I put you in a big-ass house, buy you a new car, and help you open your boutique?"

"And I appreciate that you make sure your son and I am good. However, the problem is we want to share every day with you. If that doesn't make sense to you, then I don't know how else to put it," Paris told him.

Sometime following their meals, Paris had taken Adonis to play in the kiddie pool, while Ace chilled at the table thinking shit over. He despised the thought of not being able to offer Paris and their son more of his time. But real talk, Ace did love spending time with them. He admired Paris while she stood watch over their son, and she just so happened to glance back over her shoulder, catching his eyes on her, then she playfully rolled her eyes. *Damn, she and my son deserve for a nigga to be in their lives more*, he contemplated.

Subsequent to their little pool party of three, Ace carried a sleepy Adonis up to the hotel suite, since Paris was too tired to do so. While Paris took a load off, Ace bathed Adonis, then put him in bed and he fell fast asleep. Once he had taken care of his son, it was time he took care of his girl. Ace led Paris into the large bathroom, where there was a warm bubble bath filled with red rose petals, and some lit candles placed all around the huge Jacuzzi tub, along with a bottle of champagne in a bucket of ice awaiting them. She thought the setup was absolutely beautiful. He figured she could use some of his love and affection.

Ace helped Paris out of her one-piece bathing suit and then they stepped into the tub, which was only partially filled with water. Paris sat in between Ace's legs, and they sipped champagne straight from the bottle. It was nice for them to have a moment alone.

"Bae, all that shit you said earlier did make a lot of sense," Ace told her. He sipped the champagne. "It's just—"

"Just what, Ace?" Paris intervened. "Just you're not ready to make a commitment?"

"Listen, I love your pretty-ass, Paris. You and my son is the best thing in my life. Fuck all the money, cars, clothes, and jewelry. That shit comes and goes. But I know y'all gon' always be here for me, no matter what."

"And I love you too. Me and your son need you in our lives. But sometimes your black ass act like all you care about is the streets and shit. You need to show how much you love us."

"I'll do whatever I can to do that." Ace sipped the champagne and then turned the bottle up to her lips.

"You better." Paris kissed him over her shoulder.

Ace replaced the bottle of champagne in the ice bucket and then began caressing Paris's brown skin. He played with her erect nipples, then slipped his hand in between her legs and slid two fingers inside her slit, which turned her on. She felt his dick grow to hardness then turned to face Ace and lowered her mouth onto his hard dick, she began sucking and licking on its swollen tip.

Once Ace felt himself about to bust a nut from Paris's head game, he pulled her on top and she straddled him, then grabbed his dick and slid it deep into her wet-shot. As she surf-boarded his dick, Ace palmed her ass and watched her titties jiggle. He loved the feel of her tight pussy wrapped around his hardness.

"Damn, bae... I love it so much," Ace grunted in pleasure. He leaned forward and sucked her nipples.

"Ooh, Ace, this dick feels so good!" Paris moaned. She grinded on him, allowing the full length of his dick to fill her honeypot. Bath water splashed as she rode him like a cowgirl. Ace bounced her up and down on his piece, Paris's pussy creamed all over him as she had an orgasm. "Yesss... Yesss! I'm cumming!"

Ace repositioned her on all fours while in the tub and slid deep inside of her satiny slit from behind. Paris arched her back while he fucked her, enjoying the double penetration of his big dick in her pussy and his thumb in her ass. He beat the pussy up, causing Paris to repeatedly moan his name seductively.

"Shhh, before you fuck around and wake up Adonis," Ace warned her in close to a whisper as he continued thrusting his dick balls deep into her wet-wet. The shit was so damn warm and tight, he could no longer resist bustin' a nut. "Shit, Paris!"

Following their quickie, Ace and Paris were lying in bed with their son betwixt them. While Paris and Adonis were sound asleep, Ace lay awake reflecting on the earlier discussion he'd had with Paris. He understood that she yearned for nothing more than for him to put a ring on it, but truth be told, he was married to the streets. It didn't mean he didn't care to be with Paris, because Ace knew in his heart that, unlike the streets, she was loyal to him. In addition, she had his son, and Ace loved them being a family. Although he was still creepin' on Paris with Savvy, he still felt like Paris was the one for him overall.

Looking at his girl and son lying beside him, Ace saw just how innocent they were, and couldn't stomach the thought of putting either of them in harm's way, due to his street affairs. Just because he was a certified street nigga, that didn't mean he wasn't also a family man. As much as he tried keeping his mind off of the street life while with his family, he realized the possibility of him being indicted or murdered awaited him in Milwaukee's treacherous streets. However, Ace had done his all to stay free and alive, in order to be there for his family.

Chapter 16

Ace couldn't help but to think about all of the shit he had been going through. He was in his bedroom, sitting on the floor, counting up some flip money. And he had his Glock .45 equipped with a drum and converter switch on the floor at his side. He was smoking on a Backwoods blunt full of exotic weed as he fed the money machine a stack of blue-strip hundred-dollar bills, and it made the "frrraaap" sound as it summed up yet another grand. Thus far, he had calculated forty-three thou and counting.

After removing his stash from Savvy's crib, Ace continued to add to it. He understood it was better to have his stash at home, because then he knew it was safe and sound. There was far too much paper in his stash for him not to keep a close eye on it, he had hustled too hard and put in too much work to lose it all now. Following his count up there was now seventy-two G's. In addition to the rest of his money stashed away, it all amounted to just some over one mil. Now he knew the feeling of being irritated because he had to count to a million.

Damn, I can't believe I'm a million-dollar nigga, Ace contemplated as he stashed the flip money in his safe, which was located in the closet of the master bedroom. Even though he was up a million dollars, he wouldn't forget about his hood. Most niggas hustled all of their lives until they ended up in prison for life or in a cemetery and still didn't run up a mil. But Ace had managed to do so in only a year since getting out of prison. And he had gotten rich the savage way, putting his life on the line and living by the gun. And he wanted to live long enough to enjoy his riches.

Hearing someone step into the room, Ace looked back over his shoulder and found Paris standing there. He had made her aware of his stash being in there, and even though she didn't like him having so much illegal money, drugs and firearms in their home, Paris just wanted to support Ace however she could.

"What are you up to?" Paris asked.

"Baby, lemme show you somethin'," Ace said and then turned towards the opened safe filled with plenty bundles of cash wrapped with rubber bands. "See all of this? It's what I go hard for, so I'll be able to make sure you and our son is taken care of long after I'm gone. That's a milli."

"Oh, my goodness!" Paris started screaming excitedly at the sight of a million dollars. "Ace, that's a lot of money!"

"And I'ma make sure there's a lot more." Ace pulled her close at the waist. "I know money isn't the only thing that matters, but I just don't want us to need for anything," he expressed.

"I understand that. I just want you to understand we need you far more than any amount of money," she voiced in all sincerity.

"Believe me, Paris, I most definitely understand money can't buy happiness."

"Right. Although apparently, it can buy that newest car you have outside. That thing is too much."

Ace smirked. "That thing is a Lamborghini!" He had copped himself a new toy to glaze in. "Listen, I risked my life for this money, so I'ma enjoy it while I'm still alive."

"Ace," Paris began gingerly, "just make sure you live long enough to enjoy your life with me and your son too." She kissed his lips and then exited the room, leaving him alone.

Growing up, all Ace wanted to be was a trap god, because he knew being broke wasn't for him. And now that he had made it out the trenches, it didn't mean he would switch up on his niggas. Ace couldn't help but to think about all of the L's he took. Worst of all, he hated he'd lost Gee. He wished he could have his lil bro more than any amount of money. But now all he could do is ball hard in Gee's name.

Breaking his thoughts, Ace's iPhone vibrated in the pocket of his Nike joggers. He closed the safe and then fished out the phone and saw the *FaceTime* caller was Chedda, so he answered. "Whaddup, gang?"

"Gettin' ready for the grand openin' of Baddies tonight," Chedda said. After all of the money and time invested, it was the big night for their club to finally open. "My nigga, you come scoop me up around nine pm, so we can show up at the club together."

"Bet. I'm ready for Baddies to be lit tonight."

"Fa sho. Everybody who's somebody gon' be there. Even some of our haters and opps, but that's what we got security for. Tonight, I just want for us to have a good time. Feel me?" Chedda insisted.

"Yeah, I feel you," Ace concurred. "Bro, lemme get myself together. I'ma need about an hour."

Following the call, Ace took care of his whole nine. He put on a white polo shirt with "Balenciaga" in yellow spread across the back, a pair of black OffWhite denim jeans with rips at the knees, a Balenciaga belt and sneakers. Plus, he was drippin' in his Cartier Buffalo frames and VVS diamonds on his earrings, two-tone Rolex, and thirty pointers in his new Cuban link chain straight from Gino, the jeweler. Also, he was armed with his switch on the glizzy and had a pocket full of racks. It was safe to say he was looking like a million bucks.

Ace entered the two-car garage that is connected to the house and went to his Lamborghini Murcielago. The Lamb was painted flat black, with a yellow interior and sittin' on white twenty-two-inch Rucci rims. After coppin' the whip for one-hundred-and-seventy-five G's from Shane's associate, Ace had paid Shane to have some stash spots and bulletproofed windows installed. Ace slid behind the steering wheel and roared the engine to life, then pulled out of the garage and dispelled down the street, playing Peezy's tune, "Million Dollar Nigga."

Subsequent to scoopin' up Chedda, Ace pushed the Lamb, headed for the hood to meet up with the rest of the gang. On the way, Chedda asked Ace to make a pit stop at a gas station en route. Ace pulled into the lot of a G station and parked at a vacant gas pump behind a cherry red Audi S3. Chedda stepped out and headed for the station.

While Ace sat in the Lamb rolling up a blunt of za, he peeped a familiar nigga exit the station and approach the Audi, the nigga placed the gas pump into its tank. At first glance, Ace couldn't believe it was Caine! Ace was aware the nigga had gotten out of prison about four months ago, but this was the first he had seen Caine in the streets.

Ace still remembered their last phone call and how the nigga had come at him sideways over Caine's lyin'-ass baby mama, Tia. Caine had been one of the only niggas Ace fucked with during his time in prison, and when Ace went home, like a real one, he showed love to Caine by putting cash on the phone for collect calls and dropping off cash to his BM for her to put on Caine's books. And when Tia had tried to give Ace some pussy, he turned her down and checked the hoe on the strength that she was his nigga's girl, but she had switched the story up and told Caine that Ace was the one who tried shootin' his shot at her.

Apparently, Caine had believed the conniving-ass hoe, which caused he and Ace to fall out when Caine called himself confronting Ace over some shit that actually didn't happen. And now Ace wanted to know if Caine still had beef on his mind.

Stuffing the switch on his waist, Ace lifted up the Lambo door, then hopped out of that pretty muthafucka. As he approached Caine, he peeped the stick hanging out of the pocket of Caine's jeans, and Ace was aware Caine had a rep in the streets for being savage with his too, so he kept cool but was ready to bust.

"Yo Caine, whaddup?" Ace called out in a neutral tone.

Once Caine noticed it was Ace, he grinned. "Just the nigga I been lookin' for."

"I ain't hard to find, 'cause I stay in these streets."

"Been hearin' about you out here fuckin' these streets up too, just like we used to talk about all the time when we were in the joint. A lot of niggas in that bitch talk shit about what they gon' do whenever they get out, but it takes a certain type of nigga to really do that shit. And I see you really doin' it!"

"Big facts," Ace agreed.

"Listen," Caine began tranquilly. "About that shit with Tia, I'm real enough to admit I was wrong for even comin' at you like that. You was the only nigga who kept shit so real with me once you got out. After the last time we talked on the phone, I thought about the situation like a muthafucka, and the shit just didn't sit right with me, 'cause you never gave me any reason to think you was on some fuck shit. Come to find out, Tia's ass was in these streets just givin' the pussy to all types of niggas while I was locked up. That hoe even fucked around and got pregnant by my bum-ass cousin, and now they're bums together. Feel me?

"Dawg, I ain't gon' lie, I felt so fuckin' stupid about the shit, so I couldn't even bring myself to hit your line and apologize to you then. But you was right, I had to leave that bitch alone to get my mind right. I still take care of my lil ones, but I'ont fuck with that hoe no more. Ace, just know I ain't forget about how real you kept it with me."

Ace grinned, the diamonds in his teeth dancing. "That's what real niggas do. Anyway. Good thing your fool-ass out here. It's been a long time comin', my nigga. Now you just gotta run it up to the moon."

"Fa sho. And I see you out here lookin' rich as fuck. I damn near didn't recognize your ugly ass with all those VVS diamonds in your mouth and shit." Caine admired Ace's bust-down grill, chain and watch, and also his Lamborghini.

"Had to show niggas what it looks like to be a rich savage."

"Type shit. Remember not to let hatin'-ass niggas get too close."

"That's why I mainly fuck with niggas from my hood."

"Realize that niggas from your hood will also hate on you so much, they'll try to take your place," Caine forewarned.

"I just pray I'ont have to look at one of my niggas when I gotta empty a clip," Ace told him. He noticed Chedda emerge from the station and then enter the passenger side of the Lamb. "Check it out, I gotta go and make an appearance. You should pull up to our club later tonight, Baddies."

"Yeah, I heard of that joint. Mu'fuckas say it's gonna be lit. I'll pull up fa sho."

"Cool. Good to see you out here gettin' to it, my boy."

"Same here."

After shaking up, Ace headed for his Lamb and Caine hopped into his Audi, then went on his way. It was good for Ace to have crossed paths with Caine and cleared the smoke. Ace slid behind the steering wheel and found Chedda smoking the blunt Ace had rolled.

"Who was dude?" Chedda asked, referring to Caine.

"A nigga I was locked up with," Ace said, keeping it short. He push-started the whip, then pulled out of the lot and into traffic. Soon thereafter, Ace pulled up in front of the trap spot and parked the expensive car in the hood. Bookie and Poppa was on the block with Kiki and some others. Sly was still missing in action. The group approached and admired the Lamborghini.

Bookie grinned, displaying his new gold teeth. "Damn, big bro, I see you pulled out the Lamb on niggas," he said.

"On Gee, that bitch killin' shit!" Poppa complimented.

"You stay out here glazin' on these bums," Kiki input.

"I had to jump in the Lambo like it ain't shit," Ace flexed.

Chedda chuckled. "Ace, you know we with the shits too. Now, let's slide to the club and show out."

Arriving at Baddies, Ace led the fleet of foreign whips. He veered the Lamborghini to the curb and parked directly in front of the entrance. The others parked their foreigns adjacent. When the gang stepped out of their vehicles, onlookers couldn't tell who was the richest.

The club hadn't even officially opened just yet, and already the entry line snaked down the block. Its parking lot was filled up with luxury automobiles. Baddies' grand opening had brought out some of Milwaukee's finest of all kinds. And one of the city's most prominent local rap stars, Lakeyah, was set to perform. It was sure to be a lit turnout.

Ace n'em made their way into the club, VIP status. Shortly after their arrival, the club opened for business and patrons flooded the place. Savvy and Nina had the bottle service flowing throughout the spot. And some strippers took to the stage and danced for the clubbers as they made it shower money.

The main attraction, Toy, put on one helluva show, making each of her ass cheeks clap on command and doing exclusive pole tricks. Not to mention, there were girls doing floor rounds some giving lap dances, table dances, and private dances in the champagne rooms. Plus, Lakeyah's performance had the club turnt. Thus far, the night was great.

While in the VIP section, Ace n'em sat on a huge white Italian leather wraparound couch, at a red table covered with buckets of chilled bottles and stacks of cash. Shane, Money Mel, and Sonny Boy were there receiving the VIP treatment to the fullest. Seeing that Caine had also made it to the club, Ace sent him a bottle of Ace of Spades on the house. Plenty of people approached Ace n'em table wanting to show them some love. But the gang mostly remained in their own section and turnt up.

"Is this a grand openin', or what?" Chedda said just loud enough for Ace to hear him over the music blaring from the club's subwoofers.

"Yeah, this is how it's s'posed to be," Ace replied, then poured up the bottle of Rosé to his lips.

Chedda shifted towards him. "Ace, you been my bro since we jumped off the porch. We done dodged bullets and cases together. Now I just want for us to live life without always lookin' over our damn shoulders for opps and twelve. All I'm sayin' is it's time for us to be bosses. Just look at what we have now." He gestured around the club.

"That's one-hunnit, bro. We have been through a lot of shit and finally made it out the slums together. Just know that no matter what we choose to do, it's always with a boss mentality." Ace understood real bosses had to feed their team and lead the way to the top. Although he knew that some wanted to spill the blood of a boss.

Martell "Troublesome" Bolden

Chapter 17

While out catching plays, Ace was riding in the Honda Accord. He decided to ride in Paris's old car because it wasn't conspicuous and wouldn't draw any unwarranted attention from twelve or opps. His glizzy with a switch was in his lap, and even though Ace rode in a car that was low-key, he still kept his eyes peeled for anything amiss. He had just caught his last play and was now on his way to the crib after dumpin' his entire sack for the day.

Before heading to the crib, Ace stopped at JJ's Fish & Chicken restaurant in order to grab his family some dinner. He parked in the restaurant's lot then walked inside and stood in line. While awaiting his turn to place his order, Ace pulled out his iPhone and browsed his social medias. While scrolling on *Instagram*, he unexpectedly came upon a photo Nina had posted of herself and Blue. *What the fuck is she doin' with that nigga?* Ace wondered. He didn't know what to think, but he was sure Nina could tell him where to find Blue. Ace hurried out of the restaurant and jumped into the Accord, then sped on his way.

Shortly thereafter, Ace turned onto Nina's block and peeped a nigga seated on her front porch steps, due to it being night out, he couldn't see if it was Blue. He dipped to the curb in front of Nina's crib, then hopped out of the car with his pistol in hand. The nigga sitting on the porch jumped to his feet and Ace popped the nigga twice in the chest.

Blocka, blocka!

As he stepped up on the nigga, Ace realized it wasn't Blue. Ace rushed into the house and found Nina scrambling for her phone. "Get the fuck up and stop screamin'. Shut the fuck up! Where that nigga at you posted? If you lie to me, I'ma smoke you. Matter fact, we about to get the fuck on." He grabbed her by the arm and took her phone.

"Listen, Ace, I swear I ain't do nothin' wrong," Nina cried out.

"Listen, I know. But it's somebody you know gotta go." Ace walked the bitch outside. She started screaming once she saw the body lying on the ground, so he smacked her upside the head with the gun, which caused her to bleed. He was trying to avoid her neighbors because he didn't need them to get on some police shit. He led her to the car and told her, "Drive."

"Boy, I'm bleeding. I can't see shit."

Ace made her get in the passenger seat and he would drive instead. He was sure to put the locks on child-lock as he raced down the street, because now her spot was too hot. He thought, *damn, I'm movin' way too fast.*

"Please tell me, what I did that made you mad?" Nina begged, clueless as to why Ace was doing what he was doing.

"I'm 'bout to tell you right now." Ace grabbed his phone then pulled up Blue's picture on the *'Gram* and showed her. "Tell me everything you know about this hoe-nigga, right now." Nina seen the picture and her eyes grew big. He demandingly asked, "Whassup?"

"He be shootin' shit and all his people killers," she told him, but Ace didn't give a fuck about none of that. "He took me to his house one time on 28th and Cherry Street. I'll give you the address, just don't kill me, I got children."

It was funny to Ace how this bitch wasn't thinking about them kids when she was stripping. But he knew he couldn't kill the bitch until she took him to that nigga. Even though Ace had kidnapped her, however, he felt that being around him was still a privilege. And if she did something foul, he would make sure to take her out the game on the spot.

Ace checked the gas tank and saw he needed gas. Plus, they needed something to clean up the blood, because Nina was bleeding bad. He pulled up to a gas station and parked at a pump. His heart was beating fast.

"If you make a move, that's gonna be your last," Ace warned. He stepped out, then went to buy some gas and grab some napkins. Back at the car, he gave Nina the napkins to wipe off the blood. While he pumped the gas her phone started ringing, and he saw it just so happened to be a call from Blue, then handed her the phone.

"Aye bitch, answer this. Swear you bet not panic, bitch. Pick up and talk that sexy shit."

Nina answered on speakerphone, sounding seductive. "What's the word?"

"Shit. Where you at?" Blue said. Ace knew the nigga wanted to fuck Nina with an ass so phat.

"You be playing. I been trying to see you."

"Who you with?"

"I'm with my people," was all she offered.

"Pull up on the block, I'm with the gang," he let her know.

"I'm on my way."

After ending the call, Ace took the phone back. He then put away the gas pump before hopping in the whip. Jumping back in traffic, he was on the way to slide on the hoe-ass nigga, Blue. Nina told him exactly where to go. She didn't know what the hell was going through Ace's mind, but she knew the nigga seemed like he was out of his mind. Once Ace arrived on 28th Street, he turned down the block and immediately noticed there were at least ten niggas posted outside on the sidewalk. As they rode past, Ace saw Blue posted up, wearing a dead Forty's Cuban link bust-down chain. A moment later, Nina's phone rang again, and Ace answered it on speakerphone then handed it to her.

"It's a nigga in that car with you, bitch, I just seen him. Don't ride up this block again or we gon' air that mu'fucka out!" Blue threatened.

Ace snatched the phone out of her hand, and snapped, "I'm killin' all you niggas!"

"You know where we at, just fall through, nigga!" Blue insisted, realizing the male's voice belonged to Ace. He wanted to burn Ace any fuckin' way for killing Forty, especially after Ace managed to get away the last time Blue had the drop on him.

"Say no more." Ace hung up the phone, heated as hell. He drove some blocks away and then pulled over to the curb. "My bad, Nina. This ain't got shit to do with you. I just needed to know where dawg bitch-ass was at. Here, take this." He gave her ten racks, but still had the intention to kill her ass too. "We cool?"

"Yeah. We cool," Nina assured.

"I'll see you at the club or somethin'," Ace said before pulling off on his way to the hood. He called Poppa on his way.

"Whaddup, big bro?" Poppa answered.

"Get some of the bros and plenty sticks," Ace implored him, unable to hide his anger.

"You good?"

"I just found out where the nigga Blue at who poked me. And we finna slide on him and his bitch-ass niggas right now."

"I'm with it."

Ace's other line beeped and he saw the call was from Savvy. "Look, I'll be there in a sec." He clicked over for Savvy. "Whassup, Sav?"

"Dude, what the fuck is Nina talking about? She said you snatched her up and all kinds of shit, Ace," Savvy said, sounding thrown.

"Man, listen, her ass posted a pic with the nigga that poked me. So, I just made her ass take me to the bitch-nigga."

"Ace, you didn't have to do all of that shit. Then you just kicked her out of your car, so I'm on my way to pick her ass up right now."

"I gave that bitch ten racks, so she won't trip about the shit. Just make sure her ass ain't gon' say shit."

Savvy sighed. "A'ight, Ace. You just make sure your ass stop being so damn extra."

"Sav, get the fuck off my phone with that shit. I'm on somethin' right now," he sniped before hanging up in her face.

Speeding, Ace made it to the hood in no time and parked on the block. He hopped out of the car and Poppa n'em approached him. Without saying a word, Ace went into the trap spot and grabbed a bulletproof vest and a choppa. Once Ace came out, he and the others jumped into their whips, Poppa and Bookie rode with him.

"So, how you find out where this nigga at?" Bookie inquired.

"I was lookin' through *IG* on the humbug and seen a pic of Nina and Blue she had posted on her page. So, I pulled up on that

130

bitch then snatched her ass up and made her take me to his ass. The nigga got to talkin' all greasy on the phone once he saw me in the car with the bitch. He must think he don't bleed. I can't believe how dawg was talkin'. I'ont even want the chain back, they can put it in his coffin!"

"And what about Nina?"

"Gave her ass ten G's just to keep her cool for now."

"So, where these niggas at?"

"On two-eight, right off Cherry Street. And they were at least ten deep. So, let's jump on business and kill all them niggas."

Ace n'em were strapped and vested up like the Taliban. They were war ready. Ace had the choppa, Bookie had a Glock .19 with an extended clip and a converter switch, and Poppa had an AR-15 with a square clip filled with a hundred rounds. Plus, the others from their hood, who were also all poled up, were in two separate vehicles trailing Ace n'em. Ace wanted this nigga Blue to know he wasn't lettin' no nigga take shit from him besides an L.

Once they arrived near the location, Ace pulled to a stop around the corner and the other vehicles followed suit. Ace n'em stepped out twelve-deep with guns in hand. They all crept through a back yard and jumped the gate. As Ace led the team of shooters towards the front block through the dark gangway, he held his choppa ready to tear Blue's fuckin' block up. Blue and his niggas were still posted outside, like Ace n'em wasn't coming, and there was some females present. Ace saw Blue standing there, then Ace popped outta the gangway and let the chopstick rock.

Boc, boc, boc, boc, boc, boc, boc, boc, boc, boc!

As Ace let off, his bros followed suit. Blue n'em went for their own guns, some dropped to the ground from bullets while others ran for cover as bullets chased after them. Even some of the bitches suffered bullet wounds. In the exchange of gunfire, a couple of Ace's bros were struck by flying bullets also. Rapid gunfire illuminated the dark block, bullets crashed into whatever was in the way.

Ace ran up on Blue, who was sprawled on the ground in agony after suffering three gunshots to the torso. Ace held him at gunpoint, and barked, "Bitch, what's poppin'?" He stood over that boy and looked him in the eyes, then emptied the gun.

Boc, boc, boc, boc!

Hearing sirens wailing in the distance, Ace and his boys all bounced. They each hurried back through the gangway to their vehicles and skirted off away from the crime scene.

"Y'all niggas straight?" Ace asked as he shifted the Accord through heavy traffic.

"Yeah, big bro, I'm good," Bookie said from the passenger seat.

"Me too," Poppa added while in the backseat. "But we put those bitch-ass niggas down!"

"Fa sho. Bookie, call bro n'em and see if they all good too. Here, Pop, ditch the guns." Ace wanted to make sure all his boys made it out alive, and their guns would be thrown away, so no one would be caught up with any of them and could be linked to any bodies.

Ace headed to the crib after dropping off his bros. Yielding at a stoplight, Ace grabbed his phone in order to call up Sonny Boy. He understood that even though Sonny and Blue had some bad blood between them, they were still blood brothers. And being that Sonny Boy was his nigga, he just wanted for Sonny to hear about Blue's demise from his mouth first.

"S'up, brody?" Sonny answered.

"Listen," Ace began in an easing tone. "Since you my nigga, before you hear about the shit on social media, I just wanted to be the first to let you know I stepped on Blue." There was a moment of silence, as if Sonny was paying Blue respects. "Sonny, you straight?"

"Yeah. I'm straight. Ace, I respect that you was the one to let me know, and I understand you had to do what you had to do. The shit is fucked up 'cause Blue's my brotha and you're my nigga, but I'ont play both sides. Blue picked his side, and for him it was the wrong side. So, I ain't mad at you," Sonny expressed.

"That's one-hunnid, my nigga, and I respect where you comin' from," Ace expounded. "Just know I fuck with you the long way."

"Same."

"No doubt."

Following their parting words, Ace ended the call, having more respect for Sonny Boy. He felt vindicated after smoking Blue, but it was just part of the game. Once the stoplight flipped green, he pulled off with traffic with a lot of shit on his mind.

Chapter 18

It was close to nine pm, and Ace was chillin' at the crib for the night with his girl and son. He had made it his thing to spend a couple days out the week with his family and take some time away from the streets. The family was lying on the king-sized bed inside the master bedroom, Ace and Paris shared reading a children's book to Adonis.

When Ace's iPhone vibrated on the nightstand near his bed-side, he reached over to grab it, then checked the display and saw there was a text message from Bookie. Swiping the touchscreen, Ace opened the text in order to read the message.

BOOKIE:
Me and Pop about to pull up
outside your crib. We need
to holla at u real quick.

The message seemed urgent, so Ace wondered what the fuck was up. He replied with a quick text.

ACE:
A'ight. I'll be out in a sec.

As Ace swiped "Send" on the message, he slid out of the bed and slipped on his Gucci slides. "Bae, I'm finna step outside and holla at lil bro n'em."

"What do they want with you at damn near nine at night?" Paris asked, annoyed by Ace's bros interrupting their family time.

"I'ont know. But whatever it is seems serious." Ace grabbed Paris's Gucci hoodie off the arm of the loveseat and snugged himself inside of it.

"Ace, you bet' not go nowhere with them," she insisted.

"Don't go, Daddy. Me want you to wead the book," Adonis cried out in his broken English.

"I'll be right back, boy," Ace told him.

Paris eyed Ace through slits. "Me and your son will be waiting on you."

Leaving his girl and son in bed, Ace made his way outside through the front door. He descended down the porch steps and approached Poppa's Lexus, pulled open the back door, then was greeted by thick weed smoke rushing out.

"Fuck is this about?" Ace questioned as he entered the back seat and pulled the door shut.

"Dawg, we just got word from Lisa, one of the fiends in the hood, that Sly's ass done relapsed," Bookie reported.

"What? Have y'all asked Sly if the shit is true?" Ace was thrown by the news, because from what he had been seeing lately, Sly was on top of his shit.

Poppa puffed the weed. "Not yet. But Lisa told us they used to party together back before Sly had gotten clean, and she claims that just earlier today, she ran across him at one of the trap spots. Then she says she and Sly got high together," he outlined.

"Damn. That's fucked up, bro, 'cause he was doin' good," Bookie commented.

"Hell yeah, it's fucked up. And now we can't trust his hype-ass with his hands on any more of our paper or work," Ace told them. Now he realized why Sly wasn't able to pay his debt. "Sly still owes me for a brick I fucked around and fronted him about a month back. I'm finna hit him up real quick and see if he'll answer." He pulled out his iPhone and called Sly private while on speakerphone, the line rung five times before Sly surprisingly answered. "Whassup, Sly. I see you finally answered your phone. Check it out, I got Boo and Pop here with me, and we need for you to keep shit real with us."

"Always. What is it, homeboy?" Sly inquired, sounding caught off guard.

"First off, where the fuck have your ass been at for the past week?" Ace wanted to know.

"Listen, I just been tryin' to get my mind right," he deceived. "Is that all y'all want? 'Cause I—"

Ace cut Sly short and got to the point. "Are you back smokin' that shit, Sly? 'Cause Lisa told lil bro n'em she got high with you sometime earlier today."

"Man, her punk-ass didn't tell you everything. We ain't smoke no rock out of a crack-pipe, if that's what you askin'. I just rolled up a primo blunt, that's all," Sly replied in his defense. Primo was crack-laced weed, so it was just as bad as smoking crack-rock straight from a pipe.

"Listen, Sly, that shit unacceptable," Ace objected. "Since you gettin' down like that, then me and bro don't need you handlin' no more business for us. Just cash me out that thirty bands ASAP for the shit I threw you. Afterwards, I ain't fuckin' with you like that."

"Damn, it's straight like that, huh? After all of the shit I put down with y'all, just 'cause a nigga like to party a lil bit, now y'all done fuckin' with me. That shit crazy." Sly sounded salty. He figured as long as he was only smoking primo instead of straight crack, then it wasn't a problem.

"You a good nigga and all, but we know how much that white girl can make mu'fuckas do some fucked-up shit to the ones they're close to. See how them fiends be comin' to the trap with all of their mama's and kids' shit for sale, just to chase a high. And if they'll steal from their own fam, then they'll steal from anyone," Ace expounded.

"But if a mu'fucka steal from us, that'll be the last shit he steals," Poppa input.

"No cap," Bookie seconded.

Sly scoffed. "Man, I wouldn't steal a damn thing from y'all 'cause I got my own money."

"Good to know, 'cause I'ma need you to run me that cheese you owe, so I'ont even start feelin' like you stole shit from me," Ace forewarned him.

"Oh, I see how it is. Thought we was better than that, Ace."

"Sly, I'ma give you 'til Wednesday to have that paper together for me. So that gives you three days."

"A'ight." Sly killed the call without warning. Ace shook his fuckin' head. "On what, dawg just hung up in our faces like that."

"Hype-ass nigga just salty 'cause he ain't gon' be able to eat off us no more," Boo replied.

"You mean get high off us no more," Pop corrected.

"All I know is he best have my fuckin' bread come Wednesday," Ace stated.

"Ace, the nigga probably fucked off that lil brick on some hype shit and can't even pay you back," Bookie guessed.

"Then I'ma take his Jag truck as payment, unless he gon' pay in blood. Either way, I'm gettin' paid," Ace asserted. Now he had to get the money Sly owed him, and Ace hoped that he get paid in full for Sly's sake. "Y'all niggas just make sure Sly stay away from the traps and shit."

"A'ight, we got you," Bookie assured.

"Do Chedda know about this shit too?" Ace asked.

"Not yet 'cause we pulled up on you as soon as we heard about it," Poppa answered.

"I'll let him know myself." Ace pushed open the backdoor. "Lemme get my ass back inside the crib with my bitch and son, before Paris have a damn fit. I'll get up with y'all tomorrow." He shook up with the gang before stepping out of the car.

Poppa and Bookie pulled away from the curb as Ace walked towards the house. He phoned up Chedda.

"Whaddup, gang?" Chedda picked up.

"Listen, the reason Sly haven't been around lately, is because his ass been too busy gettin' high off his own supply," Ace informed.

"How you know?"

"Dawg, lil bro n'em just pulled up on me and let me know they had heard it from Lisa. So, I called Sly and asked him and he admitted to smokin' primos, like that shit makes it better. Chedda, I ain't fuckin' with him like that no more, and I told him that we don't need him for shit else. Plus, that nigga owe me thirty G's from a front, and he gon' have to pay up ASAP."

138

"I fuck with Sly, but since he's on some junkie shit, I rather not have him around us 'cause now he's no longer trustworthy," Chedda voiced.

"Same shit I told him in other words," Ace said. He was standing on the porch about to enter the crib. "Bro, I just wanted you to be aware of what's goin' on."

"To be aware is to be alive."

"You know that," Ace agreed.

They offered their parting words before Ace ended the call. The shit concerning Sly was on the forefront of his mind, he wondered how long Sly had been smoking crack again, because Sly had done a good job at covering up his relapse. What concerned Ace the most was not knowing just how much money and yae Sly might have fucked off on the low. He couldn't help but think back to when Savvy had warned him that something about Sly had rubbed her wrong.

***

Occupying a fiend rental, Ace along with Bookie and Poppa observed a crummy bar from down the street. The block was only dimly lit by the streetlights and rain misted on this fall night.

Ace n'em were on the lookout for Sly. The day that Ace had given him to pay up had come and gone, so Ace wanted badly to run into Sly. After confronting Sly about abusing drugs and cutting him off, Ace heard word that because Lisa had exposed him, Sly pistol-whipped Lisa so brutally that she was left unrecognizable. Once it was two days past Sly's given deadline, Ace put word out that he would pay for his whereabouts. He was told that as of late, the nigga was frequenting this particular bar. Ace was thirsty to catch Sly and show him that he was deadass about being paid.

Peeping Sly's silver Jaguar SUV parked in front of the bar, it was obvious to Ace n'em that he was still inside. But Ace didn't want to barge inside the place and make a scene, so he decided to wait on the nigga to make an exit.

"Fuck all of this waitin' shit, let's just run up in that bitch and drop Sly ass," Poppa suggested. He was sitting in the back seat.

Ace looked back at him from the passenger seat and said, "Pop, just chill. I'ma do this shit my way, no guns."

"Say less. But why you wanna let this nigga live?"

"'Cause I know it's really the influence of the damn drugs that got Sly thinkin' irrational and shit. Besides, he ain't no threat."

After dropping off his bros, Ace drove on his way to Savvy's crib. He parked the fiend rental behind her house before stepping out and going inside through the back door. Making his way into the front room, he came upon Sav sitting on the couch with her brotha, Dre. Soon as Dre saw him, Ace peeped how Dre started fake clutching and mean muggin', it was obvious they didn't like each other.

"Say, my dude, fuck you doin' here?" Dre demanded as he stood to his full height. "Sis told me about how your BM pulled up on some drama, and how you came at her like I was on some snake shit. Plus, that shit you did to Nina was foul too."

"Who are you to say any fuckin' thing to me about what I got goin' on?" Ace remarked aggressively.

"Nigga, I'm—"

"Dre, I told you I got this," Savvy told her lil brotha firmly, cutting his words off. She rose onto her bare feet. "Just lemme talk to Ace myself. Why don't you go in the dining room and pour yourself a drink."

This lil nigga best listen to his big sis before I drop his ass, Ace thought bitterly as Dre mugged him while on the way into the adjacent dining room. Throwing sharp eyes at Sav, Ace stated, "So you talkin' shit about me to your lil ass brotha now? Got all my business in the streets."

Savvy folded her arms beneath her breasts and shifted her weight to one side. "It ain't even like that, Ace."

"Sounds like that to me, Sav."

"I was just talking to him about how I feel about certain shit, okay? It wasn't for him to bring it up, because I told him I would talk to you myself when I get the chance," she explained.

140

"Now's the chance. Talk," he insisted.

"Listen, Ace." Savvy took a breather to gather herself. "You know a bitch love you, but sometimes you be doing too much over the top shit. Like how you be coming at me about my brotha. I'ma be loyal to him over any other nigga. And the shit you did to my best friend wasn't even called for. Dude, you fucked Nina's face up real bad. And the crazy part is she hardly knew that nigga you was looking for. She told me that she had just met him recently, and didn't know shit about whatever beef he had with you. All you had to do was ask, but instead your ass did the most."

Ace scoffed. "You done? A'ight, now listen to this, I'ont regret shit that I choose to do. I'm a real nigga, so I can accept the shit that comes with my actions. And since you so damn loyal to your brotha over any other nigga, I can't trust your ass so I'm done fuckin' with you."

"Whatever, Ace! I'ont need you any fuckin' way!" Savvy hurled in anger.

"Bitch, you'll need me before I need you!" he retorted.

Overhearing the heated exchange of words, Dre rushed back into the front room. "Dawg, you can get the fuck outta my sis crib with that shit, or I'ma..."

Ace upped the switch then aimed it at Dre, causing him to clam up. "Or what, bitch-ass nigga? Huh?"

"Ace, just get out! Please don't shoot my brotha," Sav pled for Dre's life. She knew Ace was highly capable of catchin' a body.

"Lil nigga, I'ma spare your ass on the strength of your sista." Ace searched Dre and took the blick off his waist. Only reason he let Dre live is because he didn't want to have to smoke Savvy too. He returned his attention to her. "Sav, you'll never again meet another nigga like me."

Ace hurried out of the back door and returned to the fiend rental. He zipped out of the alley with no specific destination in mind. As he steered the car his iPhone vibrated. He figured it was Savvy calling to talk more shit, but when he checked the display, he noticed it was Bookie calling him via *FaceTime*. Answering the call, he saw Bookie was running.

"Fuck goin' on, Boo?" Ace wanted to know, perplexed.

"Dawg, shit fucked up! That nigga, Sly, came through the hood bustin' at us!" Bookie reported frantically.

"What? Y'all good? Where's Pop at?"

"Hell nah, we ain't good! That bitch-nigga popped me up, and he murked Poppa!"

Ace pulled over to the curb, needing to brace himself. "How the fuck y'all get caught slippin' like that?"

"We were chillin' on the block with Kiki n'em when Sly came out the gangway on us. Before we seen his ass comin', he started bustin'. He hit up Poppa bad, then I upped my stick and me and Sly had a pop out."

"Don't tell me that hoe-ass nigga got away."

"Nah, I left his ass stretched out on the block," Bookie told him as he hurried into his whip.

"Damn. Can't believe he smoked Poppa. What about you, are you a'ight?"

"Dawg, this shit hurt like hell. And I'm bleedin' like crazy." Bookie winced in pain.

"Bookie, maybe you should go to the hospital before you fuck around and bleed out," Ace suggested out of concern.

"I can't, 'cause right after the shots stopped, Lucas's fag-ass pulled up on the scene, so I had to get little. Now I'm on the fuckin' run for a body!"

"Shit. You gotta lay low for minute. Why don't you go to my crib, I'll be there in a sec. We gotta get you outta town ASAP."

After ending the call, Ace's mind was racing. He wasn't expecting that kind of news. In that moment he wished he had been there, perhaps Poppa would still be alive. Then again, he wasn't able to spare Gee's life, and part of him still felt some guilt about it. Losing Poppa was heavy on Ace, but he was relieved with the fact that Bookie had killed Sly in vengeance. Ace hated that he'd lost Poppa, and now Bookie was wanted for murder. Two things for certain—Ace didn't want to be the next one in a grave—or find himself in prison for the rest of his natural life.

Breaking his train of thought, Ace's iPhone vibrated once again. He saw the caller was Chedda and answered.

"Ace, dawg, you see this shit all over social media about Bookie and Poppa?" Chedda inquired, sounding perplexed.

Ace let out a heavy breath. "Yeah bro, shit crazy right now. I just got off the line with Bookie, and he told me all about it."

"Fuck happened?"

"Just pull up at my crib and we'll talk about it."

Ace dead the call and then slammed his closed fist down onto the steering wheel out of frustration. He dispelled back into traffic, speeding on his way home. Once he arrived at his house, he sat inside the fiend rental, awaiting Bookie and Chedda. Fortunately, Paris was gone with Adonis because Ace knew she would be frantic with so many damn questions, and he didn't need that shit right now.

Shortly following Ace's arrival, he saw Bookie's Lexus come weaving down the block. As Bookie faded in and out of consciousness, he managed to brake the car halfway in the street and near the curb behind the fiend rental. Ace pushed opened his door then ran over to the Lex, finding Bookie doubled over while nursing his wounds and clinging on to life. Bookie was shot four times and in hell of pain.

"You gon' be a'ight, lil bro. Just hold on," Ace encouraged him as he ripped opened the Lexus's driver's door in order to help Bookie out. He peeped the pistol laying in the passenger seat with its slide stuck on cock back from the gun being fired empty.

"Shit... I-I can't die like this," Bookie managed to say through ragged breaths.

"I ain't finna let you die. I got you."

Chedda pulled up beside them and then hastily jumped out of his Audi. He ran over to help Ace pull Bookie out of the Lex. He and Ace assisted Bookie into the backseat of the fiend rental. Then Ace instructed Chedda to quickly park the other vehicles behind his crib. After parking the Audi and Lexus behind the house then

Chedda hurried and jumped into the passenger seat of the fiend rental and Ace skirted off.

"Where the fuck we goin', Ace?" Chedda wanted to know.

"We finna take lil bro to a hospital in Kenosha. Then we gon' hide him out there in town with some of my people," Ace told him. Kenosha was a town approximately thirty minutes from Milwaukee, and Ace had people there that would assist him.

"Now tell me what the hell happened?"

"Sly got down on him and Poppa. We took that nigga whip as payment earlier today, and he came for some get-back. Bookie said he smoked the nigga after Sly killed Poppa. And that punk-ass cop Lucas knows it was lil bro, so now he's on the run," Ace filled him in. His phone was blowing up, but he ignored it.

Chedda shook his head. "This shit crazy. Let's just do whatever we can to help out lil bro." He looked into the backseat at Bookie, who was clearly in agony. Chedda personally knew how it felt to feel that fire, he'd just recently had his shit-bag officially removed after suffering gunshots himself. Chedda just hoped that Bookie would be all good. "Boo, you good back there, my nigga?"

"Dawg, this shit h-hurt like hell!" Bookie whimpered. He was in excruciating pain and felt like his wounds was burning up from the gunfire.

"We gon' get you to the hospital in no time. Just stay with us," Ace said.

Steering the car onto the highway, Ace sped on the way to Kenosha. He knew it was best to get Bookie to a hospital out of town, especially since the Milwaukee Police Department would more than likely put an APB out on him for murder. Plus, there Ace could give Bookie someplace to hideout. And thinking about Poppa being left for dead devastated him, especially after already losing Gee. Now he was hoping to at least save Bookie. He reflected back on a time when Gee, Bookie and Poppa went from babies to men. Ace just wished his young niggas would have found another way, because the streets wouldn't save them.

144

Chapter 19

Stepping out of the Lamborghini, Ace walked up to the front door of Chedda's home and pressed the Ring doorbell. He had stopped by just to check on his bro. A moment later, Chedda pulled open the door and Ace entered the plush house. Ace acknowledged Chedda's fiancé, Antionette, and their two girls, Londyn and Jordyn, who were all in the living room. He followed Chedda into the master bedroom, where Ace noticed there were three bricks sitting out on the bed, along with a Glock .19 and a pair of thirty-shot sticks.

"S'up, my nigga," Ace greeted.

"I'm a'ight. You?" Chedda replied. He collected a backpack from the closet, then placed the kilos inside.

"Still tryin' to get my mind off all of this shit that has taken place lately. So I'ma take my girl and son to a Bucks game tonight."

"That's whassup. It's only right that we spend as much time with our families, 'cause tomorrows ain't guaranteed in this game we playin'. Feel me?"

"Yeah, I feel you without a doubt, my boy," Ace replied. After all of the drama that had unfolded over time, he felt like at any given time he could be next. "Speakin' of the game, I see you got bricks on deck."

"Yeah. I'm 'bout to go and make a serve real quick. Rex coppin' two birds, and I told him I'll front him another one," Chedda informed.

"Then I'ma ride with you, just in case you need some A.A. with that much product on the line."

"No need, fam. You know I keep at least a thirty-shot on me." Chedda grinned and grabbed his Glock, attached one of the extended clips onto it, then put the gun on his waist.

"Since when did Rex start coppin' birds?" Ace inquired suspiciously.

"Guess he's really tryna get his weight up in the game. We both know that shit takes time."

Ace scoffed. "Part of me just don't trust dawg, 'cause I think the nigga is suspect."

"Rex has been one of my most trusted buyers for a long time now. Stop trippin'. Besides, this will be my last run. After I serve these bricks then I'm done gettin' my hands dirty, I'ma just focus on runnin' our strip club. Ace, this street shit ain't for me no more, I got a fiancée and two lil girls to look after. And you should be thinkin' the same. 'Cause we both know how this shit ends, with us either in prison or dead," Chedda expressed.

"I respect that, Chedda. And you of all people know I'ma do what I gotta to look after my bitch and shorties. But the streets is all I know, so I'ma keep the business in the streets goin' while you clean up the money through the club. We in this shit together," Ace expounded.

"Fa sho," Chedda agreed. He knew Ace was a pure street-nigga and wouldn't shit change that, so he respected where Ace was coming from as well. "Just don't forget that we're the only two who are left in this shit. Look at how the game has taken our niggas away from us without remorse. Gee and Poppa took it in slugs, Bookie is on the run for his life, and Sly fell vic to the dope again. Not to mention that you and I have already barely evaded prison and death. But who knows how long that will continue to last for us, 'cause the game ain't loyal."

"Chedda, we all we got now. So, we gotta watch each other's backs. It's fucked up that most of the real ones are either dead or in prison, but we gon' make it."

Things were now much different in Ace and Chedda's lives. It was crazy how they had gone from babies to men. The two used to talk about all of the shit they was gonna make happen, but they didn't realize how much shit they would have to go through.

Chedda's iPhone rang and he saw the call was from Rex, who was awaiting him. He grabbed the backpack and Ace trailed him into the living room. After Chedda kissed all three of his girls goodbye, he assured them he would be back later. Once outside, Ace and Chedda stood on the sidewalk near their Lamb and Benz-Jeep, parked at the curb. The weather still felt good, although the

146

leaves on the trees started to change colors, due to it inching towards fall.

"Look, lemme go and dump these bricks real quick," Chedda told him.

"Bro, you sure you don't want me to ride with you?" Ace asked.

"I'll be good. Just go ahead and have a good time with your family, bro."

"Hit my line if you need me."

"A'ight. I will," Chedda assured. "Plenty much love."

"Never enough," Ace responded genuinely.

The two shook up the rakes and then stepped into their perspective whips, going separate ways. Ace was headed home, while Chedda went on his way to meet with Rex to make his last run.

Ace rode to EST Gee's tune, "Bigger Than Life or Death." He thought, *It's hard for me to make it out 'cause the streets got a hold on me. With opps and twelve trying to take me out, I have to keep a gun on me and be vigilant. It's fucked up how I came up in the hood where fiends roam, slugs fly, and niggas shoot dice in the gangways, and most of the residents can't bet on a nine-to-five so their only resort is to scam, hit licks and make plays.*

I remember the time when me and bro n'em only had crack rocks, until we stacked enough paper to cop a key from the plug. All of my life I got it out the mud and put in dirty work by trappin', hittin' licks, and puttin' in gun work. I seen a lot of young niggas get murked on the average, and quickly realized niggas barely live to be twenty-one if they're not a savage. I was chasin' street dreams while niggas was sleepin' on me, and federal nightmares still got my ass afraid of bein' caught up in a fed sweep.

Damn, I'll never forget me and my siblings havin' to grow up on mayonnaise sandwiches 'cause our mama wasn't really there for us and our pops was killed early on. So, I was raised by the streets, where it's either kill or be killed because there isn't any other options. I've seen lots of niggas catch a slug, lots of niggas catch a case, and I know that breakin' the G-code is the only way niggas would catch a break. I think of how me and my niggas used to be posted on the corner, tryin' to move a sack with the under-standin' that it was death around the corner, so we was down to shoot it out.

And once I really started gettin' money then it didn't cause me to change up. But more money bred more problems, so it really didn't change shit for me. 'Cause now more than ever, I got bitches tryin' to finesse me, niggas out to kill me, and twelve thirsty to indict me, when all I'm tryin' to do is take care of my family.

Thus far, I've been through hell and back, from bein' broke to bein' popped, to bein' to prison. And I can't believe those aren't even the worst things, the worst is havin' flashbacks about my brother's murder. However, I have to make the best of life 'til the death of me.

Arriving at home, Ace parked curbside. He made his entrance through the front door of the house and came upon Adonis sitting on the couch in the front room while watching TV. On his way towards the master bedroom, Ace rubbed his son's peanut head. Inside the room he found Paris's sexy ass lying on their king-sized bed while on her iPhone doing some online shopping. She observed him remove his Glock and take off his Kevlar vest then place both items within his top sock drawer. A huge part of her wished that one day he wouldn't have to live his life always ready to ride or die. Ace sat on edge of the bed beside Paris and pecked her on the lips and gingerly rubbed her cheek.

"Stop kissing me, because that's how we got this second child on the way," Paris half-joked.

"Girl, I'll kiss you when I want. And you mean to tell me you're pregnant?" Ace wanted to know.

She nodded. "I'm six weeks along. I've been wanting to tell you, but there's been so much going on lately."

"Damn, bae, I didn't even notice." Now Ace understood why Paris was pressing him about marriage lately.

"Didn't you notice me eating more than usual?" Paris pointed out.

"Don't try to blame your appetite on my baby." He chuckled.

148

Paris playfully pushed him. "Whatever, you play too much! But for real, Ace, do you think we're ready for another child? Because I'll admit I'm afraid."

"Listen, there's no need for you to be afraid of us havin' another lil one. Especially since you're already a good mom to Adonis. Plus, you know I'ma be here for y'all." Ace peeped that she diverted her eyes away from him. "What's wrong, bae?"

"It's just that with Adonis growing up so fast—he think he's grown already—and this baby on the way, I need you now more than ever before. More importantly, our kids need their father," she expressed emotionally.

"Dude, you and my lil ones are my prized possessions in life, and I'ma cherish y'all 'til the death of me. I know I haven't always been some type of perfect nigga, but I have always been here," he expounded sincerely. "Yes, you have. And I love you for that."

"Luh you too."

Ace leaned in and kissed Paris with passion. He slid his hand beneath her shirt and fondled her titties. She felt herself growing wet between the legs. Ace helped Paris out of her shirt and began licking her hard nipples.

"Hold on, baby. Adonis may walk in on us," Paris reminded him.

"I'ma make this quick. But if it makes you feel better, I'll lock the door." Ace went and locked the bedroom door, then he returned to the bed with Paris. He wasted no time pulling off her biker shorts, revealing her trimmed kitty. While she was seated on the edge of the bed with her legs agape, Ace knelt before her and put his mouth to work on her pussy. As he flicked his warm tongue over her clit, Ace pulled down his joggers and set free his hard dick. She leaned back and watched as Ace pleasured her orally.

"Oooohh... Mmm... Yesss, baby, yesss!" Paris moaned softly. She loved the way he made her feel sexually and emotionally. Ace wasn't perfect by far, although she appreciated that he did his best to show her just how much he loved her. "Dammit... I'm finna... cummm!" As Ace finger-fucked her twat, he sucked on her pussy lips and Paris's toes curled. The feel of his warm tongue and its rapid motions caused her to reach climax, and Ace lapped up her juices.

Rising to his feet, Ace slowly slid his hardness in her slit while she remained lying back on edge of the bed. He pushed her knees towards her chest and stroked her deeply, hitting her G-spot. Damn, he loved how she made him feel. His feelings for her were genuine, and even though he wasn't perfect, that didn't mean he wasn't good for her. "Mm, babygirl... this pussy so fuckin' wet," Ace groaned in pleasure. He was caught up in a trance from the feel of her slit wrapped around his wood as she came again.

Paris pushed him back and then turned around and positioned herself on all fours, he climbed in bed behind her then she reached back and grabbed his hardness and guided it inside of her satiny twat. "Now fuck me," she demanded. While holding her ass steady, Ace sped up his thrusts as he buried his love tool in her wet-shot while she arched her back. It turned him on most when she looked back over her shoulder at him, who was biting down on his lower lip, while he beat the pussy up and gripped the satin sheets.

"Oh, shit... I'm finna bust a nut!" Ace was no longer able to hold back a nut as Paris threw the pussy back on him, he pulled his dick out and skeeted on her ass. He rolled over in bed beside her, both panting. "Boo, that wet was so fuckin' good."

"And it's all yours." Paris grabbed his limp dick in her petite, pedicure hand. "This better be all mine."

Ace grinned. "It's enough of it go around."

"What?"

"I'm just fuckin' with you, bae," he laughed.

Paris playfully punched his chest. "Ugh. Boy, you play too much."

"Don't worry, Paris. All this dick belongs to you." Ace really wanted to be faithful to Paris moving forward after he had dumped Savvy. He realized Paris loved him unconditionally and was loyal to him overall. "C'mon, let's get ready to go to the Bucks game."

Subsequent to Ace n'em getting ready, the entire family was dressed in Milwaukee Bucks attire to represent their home team.

Ace had on a Bucks championship snapback cap, Paris wore a female Mitchell & Ness throwback Kareem Abdul-Jabbar Bucks jersey with her slight baby bump showing, and Adonis sported a toddler T-shirt with the Bucks mascot on it.

As they were finna leave out of the house, Paris noticed Ace grab his gun from the drawer. "Dude, you don't have to always have that with you," she told him, and Ace knew she was referring to the gun.

"Rather be caught dead with it than without it," he replied.

Paris sighed. "Listen, can we please just have one normal night out as a family?"

Ace understood that she didn't know the half of the beef he had in the streets, so she didn't quite get why the gun was necessary. He didn't like the idea of being naked without a gun, but he decided to leave it in order to please her. "A'ight, I'll leave it."

Once the family headed out of the house, they then entered Ace's Lamb, Ace slid behind the steering wheel while Paris secured Adonis on her lap once entering the passenger side of the two-seater. They set off to the Fiserv Forum arena for the Milwaukee Bucks NBA game. Arriving downtown, they made it to the arena. After parking the Lamb in a private lot, the family headed inside the arena for the sporting event.

During tipoff of the basketball game, Ace and his family found their floor seats, where they were sitting courtside and would be watching the game up close and personal. Seated to the left of them was the famous Milwaukee rap artist, Lakeyah, with her entourage, and just to their right was the Bucks team bench. The place was sold out and the fans were live as they cheered on the home team. As the game played on, Paris pulled out her iPhone, then snapped some pictures of herself with Ace and their son having a good time and posted it on her social medias.

Ace also took live video for his social medias of the Bucks superstar, Giannis Antetokounmpo, going up for a slam dunk over an opposing defensive player, and the arena went wild! At one point the superstar dove into Ace as the athlete saved the basketball from going out of bounds. The game was filled with excitement.

Once it was halftime, Ace n'em watched as the Bucks mascot, Bango, used a trampoline to do some aerodynamic slam dunks, which Adonis liked most. The kiss cam landed on Ace and Paris, so they kissed on live TV while Adonis sat between them. And the Bucks cheerleaders took to the floor and began performing a dance routine. Shortly after, the game resumed, and the home team won. Subsequent to the Bucks game, Ace and his family were back in traffic, heading home.

"Adonis, did you have fun at the game?" Paris asked.

"Yep, Mommy!" Adonis exclaimed.

"Good." Paris glanced over at Ace, who was busy texting. "And who are you texting right now?"

"It's my ma. I gotta make a stop by her crib before we go home," Ace said.

"She okay?"

"Yeah. She just wanna see me real quick."

"Alright. It'll be nice to see her."

Soon thereafter, they pulled up to Gale's house. Ace parked at the curb near Gee's shrine then they stepped out of the car. He noticed Reverend Johnson seated out on his porch, who offered a wave as Ace made his way for the house. Paris grabbed Adonis and followed Ace. Upon entering the house Ace found Gale, Mika, and Kiki in the front room. Adonis ran along to play with Mika's son, Breon.

"Whassup, y'all," Ace greeted them.

"Hey, son," Gale replied. She was seated on the couch. "We're just reminiscing about your brother, and I just wanted you to be here with us."

"Bro, I was just telling Mama about how much Glen looked up to you," Mika chimed in from the seat beside her mom.

"Yeah, Gee spoke highly about Ace all of the time," Kiki input.

Ace took a seat on the arm of the couch. "Lil bro was a real nigga. I miss him every day, and part of me still blame myself for his death." He still couldn't help but get emotional whenever he thought of Gee.

"Bae, your little brother knows how much you love him," Paris assured as she rubbed his back in solace.

"He knows that all of us miss and love him," Gale piped in. "So, let's remember the good times with him."

They all reminisced about good times they shared with Glen. Just hearing the stories made them all miss him so much more.

"On a lighter note," Ace chimed in. "Me and Paris have another lil one on the way."

"I'm so happy for y'all!" Kiki exclaimed.

"Me too, bro," Mika seconded.

"The more grandkids the better," Gale added.

Paris smiled. "Thank y'all. I just hope that now Ace black-ass realizes how significant it is for him to be with his family."

"Trust me, I realize family is everything. That's why I'ma do my all to be here with y'all," Ace assured.

Gale wanted for Ace to see the bigger picture. "Son, family is everything, it's the only thing."

In that moment, Ace's iPhone buzzed and he peeped it was a call from Antoinette. *She must be callin' me to see where Chedda is*, he mused. Stepping into the kitchen away from the others, he answered the call. "S'up, Nett."

"Oh, my God, Ace! The feds got Chedda!" Nett told him in a panic.

"What?! How do you know this?"

"He just called me from the precinct. And he wanted me to let you know you was right about someone named Rex," she reported.

Unbeknownst to Chedda, Rex had been working with the feds to build a case on him. For some time now, the feds were watching Chedda's every move, and they had his phones wiretapped. After Rex had gotten jammed up with a half-brick of cooked crack a while ago, in order to cut a deal with the feds, he mentioned Chedda's name as his plug. And so far, the feds had accumulated almost ten kilos worth of dope through each time Chedda had served Rex. The most unfortunate part was this serve was supposed to be Chedda's last run.

Ace shook his damn head and heatedly thought, *Somethin' told me that nigga, Rex, was workin' with the alphabet boys. I just wish Chedda would've listened to me. Now I gotta do whatever I can to help my nigga.* "Listen, don't say no more on the phone. I'm pull up on you," he told her. Ace ended the call, figuring more than likely, the feds had his phone wiretapped. It was fucked up how shit was going bad for him and all of his niggas. Once Ace returned to the front room, the others could read that something was wrong with him.

"Is everything okay, bro?" Mika inquired.

"That was Nett. She let me know the feds snatched up Chedda," he informed.

Gale knew the feeling of being indicted all too well. "If they got him, then there's not much he can do but keep his lips sealed and just accept his time."

"I have no doubt he'll do that, bein' the real nigga he is. Look, I gotta go check on Nett."

After saying their goodbyes, Ace n'em headed out. Ace approached the Lamborghini and lifted up the passenger door for Paris, then she and Adonis got into the car before Ace entered the driver's side. As Ace push-started the car, suddenly, an unmarked Dodge Magnum drew up with its police lights flickering and screeched to a halt partially in front of the Lamb, blocking it off. The dirty cops, Lucas and Bradshaw, jumped out of the unmarked vehicle and ran up on the car pointing their guns, not wanting to allow Ace to get away because he was wanted for a slew of felonious crimes, ranging from drugs to murders.

Ace had always promised himself that before he went back to jail, he would rather hold court in the streets, but he didn't have his gun on him to put up any objections.

"Police! Freeze! Turn off the car, put your hands on the wheel, and don't move!" Lucas demanded while holding Ace at gunpoint. And Bradshaw hovered over the passenger side.

"Shit," Ace cursed, taken by surprise.

"Ace, what's going on?" Paris wanted to know frantically.

"The police have been after me for a while now. They wanna question me."

"For what?"

Ace looked at her with sorrowful eyes. "Dope and bodies."

"Me scared, Daddy!" Adonis cried.

"Don't worry, son, it's gon' be all good," Ace told him. He took a deep breath as he thought about the situation at hand. Part of him wanted to flee and make the cops catch him if they could, but looking at his girl and son, he didn't care to put them in any danger. So, he decided to go ahead and turn himself in, with the hopes he would beat any charges. "Paris, I'm finna turn myself in, and I'ont know if I'll ever see y'all again. Listen, I want you to know I love you and Adonis." Ace looked at his son. "Make sure you take care of your mama. I gotta go for now, hopefully I'll be back soon."

"We love you too, Ace. Just do what you have to do," Paris told him. She pulled out her iPhone and began filming, just in case there was any police brutality.

By now there was a crowd of onlookers gathered outside watching the scene unfold, most of whom were familiar with how the two crooked cops had it out for Ace. Gale, Mika, and Kiki were all standing on the porch.

"Driver, slowly step out of the vehicle. Now!" Bradshaw barked his order.

Ace offed the engine. He took a deep breath, then pushed open the door and started to step out of the car.

"Gun!" Lucas called out, then opened fire.

Boom, boom, boom, boom, boom!

Ace fell back into the interior of the car as he was riddled with a barrage of bullets. He was shot five times in the stomach, four in the chest, and once in his neck. His breaths quickened and blood poured from his wounds and filled his lungs as he faded in and out of consciousness.

"Noooo!" Paris screamed at the top of her lungs, having just witnessed Ace be shot up. She reached over to check on him while continuing to film on her phone. "Ace, baby, just breathe. Stay with me, baby!"

"Daddy!" Adonis cried and reached out for his dad, seeing him bleeding profusely.

Mika and Kiki held Gale back as she tried to run over to Ace. "Not my son, not like this!" Gale wailed.

As Ace gasped for air and fought for his life, his family and friends were forced to observe him slowly dying. Reverend Johnson shouted for someone to call the paramedics. He couldn't believe that he had just witnessed the police shoot yet another unarmed Black man. What's even sadder is the fact that Rev had always known that one day, he would have to bury Ace in an early grave.

And even though it was actually no gun in Ace's hand but a cellphone instead, a major part of Lucas felt justified in shooting him. It was all too normal for cops to shoot and kill unarmed Black men and women only to get away with murder due to social injustice and systemic racism, and now Ace was a victim of those unfortunate and bias circumstances. Of all ways to go, who knew Ace would die by a cop's gun.

Ace's young life began to flash before his eyes, he thought about everything he had done, the good and bad. He thought about what Paris meant to him and how much he loved her and their son, and not being able to be there for his unborn child. He thought about how Gee must have felt, knowing his life was finna end, and wondered if he would see his brother in the afterlife. He thought about all of the money he had made and the fact that he couldn't take it to the grave with him. He thought about all of the niggas he had murdered and didn't regret it. He thought about what his life meant to him, and remembered Rev asking him if he cared whether he live to be old or die young.

Back then, he had told Rev it didn't matter, only because he had witnessed so many niggas live fast and die young in the streets, so it almost seemed like his fate. However, now that he was on the verge of losing his life at such a young age, with his final breath he thought, *I ain't ready to die....*

Epilogue

In the wake of Ace being unjustly murdered, the video Paris had posted on social media of yet another cop shooting an unarmed Black man to death sparked a worldwide protest. People from all walks of life were gathered in the streets with signs and bullhorns letting the world know that *Black Lives Matter*. There was an outpour of love for Ace, so much so that *#JusticeForAce* was trending on social media.

Some of the biggest names in the Black community spoke out about the unjust murder, including former President Barack Obama. It was a similar movement to those after the unjust murders of Trayvon Martin, Tamir Rice, Eric Garner, Mike Brown, Philando Castile, Ezell Ford, Ahmad Arbery, Jayland Walker, Breona Taylor, and George Floyd, to name a few.

The Milwaukee Police Department was exposed for their systemic racism, and Detectives Lucas and Bradshaw were both fired from the force, then indicted for murder. And eventually they were found guilty of murder after trial and sentenced to twenty-five years imprisonment. Also, Ace's loved ones had sued the department and won a settlement of a few million dollars. Although the money would help take care of them, it wouldn't bring back Ace.

His family and friends had to find a way to live on without him. It was his son, Adonis, who was affected by his dad's death most. Ace knew what it had been like to grow up without his own dad, so Ace always wanted to be there for his own son, to teach him to be a better man than himself. More than anything, Ace wanted for his son to be the one to break the cycle of becoming a statistic. As for his unborn child, Paris had a miscarriage due to stress.

As for the others, Chedda was indicted under the RICO Act, he was eventually found guilty and sentenced to federal prison for thirty years. And Bookie was wanted for Sly's murder, and he was still on the run. The street life had claimed Ace and all of his gang in one way or another. However, in the streets of Milwaukee where Ace had made a name for himself, he would forever be remembered as a rich savage.

The End...

Lock Down Publications and Ca$h Presents assisted
publishing packages.

BASIC PACKAGE $499
Editing
Cover Design
Formatting

UPGRADED PACKAGE $800
Typing
Editing
Cover Design
Formatting

ADVANCE PACKAGE $1,200
Typing
Editing
Cover Design
Formatting
Copyright registration
Proofreading
Upload book to Amazon

LDP SUPREME PACKAGE $1,500
Typing
Editing
Cover Design
Formatting
Copyright registration
Proofreading
Set up Amazon account
Upload book to Amazon
Advertise on LDP Amazon and Facebook page

***Other services available upon request. Additional charges may apply

Lock Down Publications
P.O. Box 944
Stockbridge, GA 30281-9998
Phone # 470 303-9761

Submission Guideline

Submit the first three chapters of your completed manuscript to ldpsubmissions@gmail.com, subject line: Your book's title. The manuscript must be in a .doc file and sent as an attachment. Document should be in Times New Roman, double spaced and in size 12 font. Also, provide your synopsis and full contact information. If sending multiple submissions, they must each be in a separate email.

Have a story but no way to send it electronically? You can still submit to LDP/Ca$h Presents. Send in the first three chapters, written or typed, of your completed manuscript to:

LDP: Submissions Dept
Po Box 944
Stockbridge, Ga 30281

DO NOT send original manuscript. Must be a duplicate.

Provide your synopsis and a cover letter containing your full contact information.

Thanks for considering LDP and Ca$h Presents.

<u>NEW RELEASES</u>

KILLA KOUNTY by KHUFU

BETRAYAL OF A THUG 2 by FRE$H

THE COCAINE PRINCESS 5 by KING RIO

FOR THE LOVE OF BLOOD 2 by JAMEL MITCHELL

RICH $AVAGE 3 by MARTELL "TROUBLESOME" BOLDEN

BLOOD OF A BOSS **VI**

SHADOWS OF THE GAME II

TRAP BASTARD II

By **Askari**

LOYAL TO THE GAME **IV**

By **T.J. & Jelissa**

TRUE SAVAGE **VIII**

MIDNIGHT CARTEL IV

DOPE BOY MAGIC IV

CITY OF KINGZ III

NIGHTMARE ON SILENT AVE II

THE PLUG OF LIL MEXICO II

CLASSIC CITY II

By **Chris Green**

BLAST FOR ME **III**

A SAVAGE DOPEBOY III

CUTTHROAT MAFIA III

DUFFLE BAG CARTEL VII

HEARTLESS GOON VI

By **Ghost**

A HUSTLER'S DECEIT III

KILL ZONE II

BAE BELONGS TO ME III

TIL DEATH II

By **Aryanna**

KING OF THE TRAP III

By **T.J. Edwards**

GORILLAZ IN THE BAY V

3X KRAZY III

STRAIGHT BEAST MODE III
De'Kari
KINGPIN KILLAZ IV
STREET KINGS III
PAID IN BLOOD III
CARTEL KILLAZ IV
DOPE GODS III
Hood Rich
SINS OF A HUSTLA II
ASAD
YAYO V
Bred In The Game 2
S. Allen
THE STREETS WILL TALK II
By Yolanda Moore
SON OF A DOPE FIEND III
HEAVEN GOT A GHETTO II
SKI MASK MONEY II
By Renta
LOYALTY AIN'T PROMISED III
By Keith Williams
I'M NOTHING WITHOUT HIS LOVE II
SINS OF A THUG II
TO THE THUG I LOVED BEFORE II
IN A HUSTLER I TRUST II
By Monet Dragun
QUIET MONEY IV
EXTENDED CLIP III
THUG LIFE IV
By **Trai'Quan**

THE STREETS MADE ME IV

By **Larry D. Wright**

IF YOU CROSS ME ONCE II

ANGEL V

By **Anthony Fields**

THE STREETS WILL NEVER CLOSE IV

By **K'ajji**

HARD AND RUTHLESS III

KILLA KOUNTY IV

By **Khufu**

MONEY GAME III

By **Smoove Dolla**

JACK BOYS VS DOPE BOYS IV

A GANGSTA'S QUR'AN V

COKE GIRLZ II

COKE BOYS II

LIFE OF A SAVAGE V

CHI'RAQ GANGSTAS V

By **Romell Tukes**

MURDA WAS THE CASE III

Elijah R. Freeman

THE STREETS NEVER LET GO III

By **Robert Baptiste**

AN UNFORESEEN LOVE IV

BABY, I'M WINTERTIME COLD II

By **Meesha**

MONEY MAFIA II

By **Jibril Williams**

QUEEN OF THE ZOO III

By **Black Migo**

VICIOUS LOYALTY III

By **Kingpen**

A GANGSTA'S PAIN III

By **J-Blunt**

CONFESSIONS OF A JACKBOY III

By **Nicholas Lock**

GRIMEY WAYS III

By **Ray Vinci**

KING KILLA II

By **Vincent "Vitto" Holloway**

BETRAYAL OF A THUG III

By **Fre$h**

THE MURDER QUEENS III

By **Michael Gallon**

THE BIRTH OF A GANGSTER III

By **Delmont Player**

TREAL LOVE II

By **Le'Monica Jackson**

FOR THE LOVE OF BLOOD III

By **Jamel Mitchell**

RAN OFF ON DA PLUG II

By **Paper Boi Rari**

HOOD CONSIGLIERE III

By **Keese**

PRETTY GIRLS DO NASTY THINGS II

By **Nicole Goosby**

PROTÉGÉ OF A LEGEND II

By **Corey Robinson**

IT'S JUST ME AND YOU II

By Ah'Million
BORN IN THE GRAVE II
By Self Made Tay
FOREVER GANGSTA III
By Adrian Dulan
GORILLAZ IN THE TRENCHES II
By SayNoMore
THE COCAINE PRINCESS VI
By King Rio

Available Now

RESTRAINING ORDER **I & II**
By **CA$H & Coffee**
LOVE KNOWS NO BOUNDARIES **I II & III**
By **Coffee**
RAISED AS A GOON I, II, III & IV
BRED BY THE SLUMS I, II, III
BLAST FOR ME I & II
ROTTEN TO THE CORE I II III
A BRONX TALE I, II, III
DUFFLE BAG CARTEL I II III IV V VI
HEARTLESS GOON I II III IV V
A SAVAGE DOPEBOY I II

DRUG LORDS I II III
CUTTHROAT MAFIA I II
KING OF THE TRENCHES
By **Ghost**
LAY IT DOWN **I & II**
LAST OF A DYING BREED I II
BLOOD STAINS OF A SHOTTA I & II III
By **Jamaica**
LOYAL TO THE GAME I II III
LIFE OF SIN I, II III
By **TJ & Jelissa**
BLOODY COMMAS I & II
SKI MASK CARTEL I II & III
KING OF NEW YORK I II,III IV V
RISE TO POWER I II III
COKE KINGS I II III IV V
BORN HEARTLESS I II III IV
KING OF THE TRAP I II
By **T.J. Edwards**
IF LOVING HIM IS WRONG…I & II
LOVE ME EVEN WHEN IT HURTS I II III
By **Jelissa**
WHEN THE STREETS CLAP BACK I & II III
THE HEART OF A SAVAGE I II III IV
MONEY MAFIA
LOYAL TO THE SOIL I II III
By **Jibril Williams**
A DISTINGUISHED THUG STOLE MY HEART I II & III
LOVE SHOULDN'T HURT I II III IV
RENEGADE BOYS I II III IV

PAID IN KARMA I II III
SAVAGE STORMS I II III
AN UNFORESEEN LOVE I II III
BABY, I'M WINTERTIME COLD
By **Meesha**
A GANGSTER'S CODE I &, II III
A GANGSTER'S SYN I II III
THE SAVAGE LIFE I II III
CHAINED TO THE STREETS I II III
BLOOD ON THE MONEY I II III
A GANGSTA'S PAIN I II
By J-Blunt
PUSH IT TO THE LIMIT
By **Bre' Hayes**
BLOOD OF A BOSS **I, II, III, IV, V**
SHADOWS OF THE GAME
TRAP BASTARD
By **Askari**
THE STREETS BLEED MURDER **I, II & III**
THE HEART OF A GANGSTA I II& III
By **Jerry Jackson**
CUM FOR ME I II III IV V VI VII VIII
An **LDP Erotica Collaboration**
BRIDE OF A HUSTLA **I II & II**
THE FETTI GIRLS **I, II& III**
CORRUPTED BY A GANGSTA I, II III, IV
BLINDED BY HIS LOVE
THE PRICE YOU PAY FOR LOVE I, II ,III
DOPE GIRL MAGIC I II III
By **Destiny Skai**

WHEN A GOOD GIRL GOES BAD

By **Adrienne**

THE COST OF LOYALTY I II III

By Kweli

A GANGSTER'S REVENGE **I II III & IV**

THE BOSS MAN'S DAUGHTERS I II III IV V

A SAVAGE LOVE **I & II**

BAE BELONGS TO ME I II

A HUSTLER'S DECEIT I, II, III

WHAT BAD BITCHES DO I, II, III

SOUL OF A MONSTER I II III

KILL ZONE

A DOPE BOY'S QUEEN I II III

TIL DEATH

By **Aryanna**

A KINGPIN'S AMBITON

A KINGPIN'S AMBITION **II**

I MURDER FOR THE DOUGH

By **Ambitious**

TRUE SAVAGE I II III IV V VI VII

DOPE BOY MAGIC I, II, III

MIDNIGHT CARTEL I II III

CITY OF KINGZ I II

NIGHTMARE ON SILENT AVE

THE PLUG OF LIL MEXICO II

CLASSIC CITY

By **Chris Green**

A DOPEBOY'S PRAYER

By **Eddie "Wolf" Lee**

THE KING CARTEL **I, II & III**

By **Frank Gresham**

THESE NIGGAS AIN'T LOYAL **I, II & III**

By **Nikki Tee**

GANGSTA SHYT **I II &III**

By **CATO**

THE ULTIMATE BETRAYAL

By **Phoenix**

BOSS'N UP **I , II & III**

By **Royal Nicole**

I LOVE YOU TO DEATH

By **Destiny J**

I RIDE FOR MY HITTA

I STILL RIDE FOR MY HITTA

By **Misty Holt**

LOVE & CHASIN' PAPER

By **Qay Crockett**

TO DIE IN VAIN

SINS OF A HUSTLA

By **ASAD**

BROOKLYN HUSTLAZ

By **Boogsy Morina**

BROOKLYN ON LOCK I & II

By **Sonovia**

GANGSTA CITY

By **Teddy Duke**

A DRUG KING AND HIS DIAMOND I & II III

A DOPEMAN'S RICHES

HER MAN, MINE'S TOO I, II

CASH MONEY HO'S

THE WIFEY I USED TO BE I II

PRETTY GIRLS DO NASTY THINGS
By Nicole Goosby
TRAPHOUSE KING **I II & III**
KINGPIN KILLAZ I II III
STREET KINGS I II
PAID IN BLOOD **I II**
CARTEL KILLAZ I II III
DOPE GODS I II
By **Hood Rich**
LIPSTICK KILLAH **I, II, III**
CRIME OF PASSION I II & III
FRIEND OR FOE I II III
By **Mimi**
STEADY MOBBN' **I, II, III**
THE STREETS STAINED MY SOUL I II III
By **Marcellus Allen**
WHO SHOT YA **I, II, III**
SON OF A DOPE FIEND I II
HEAVEN GOT A GHETTO
SKI MASK MONEY
Renta
GORILLAZ IN THE BAY **I II III IV**
TEARS OF A GANGSTA I II
3X KRAZY I II
STRAIGHT BEAST MODE I II
DE'KARI
TRIGGADALE I II III
MURDAROBER WAS THE CASE I II
Elijah R. Freeman
GOD BLESS THE TRAPPERS I, II, III

THESE SCANDALOUS STREETS I, II, III
FEAR MY GANGSTA I, II, III IV, V
THESE STREETS DON'T LOVE NOBODY I, II
BURY ME A G I, II, III, IV, V
A GANGSTA'S EMPIRE I, II, III, IV
THE DOPEMAN'S BODYGAURD I II
THE REALEST KILLAZ I II III
THE LAST OF THE OGS I II III
Tranay Adams
THE STREETS ARE CALLING
Duquie Wilson
MARRIED TO A BOSS I II III
By Destiny Skai & Chris Green
KINGZ OF THE GAME I II III IV V VI
Playa Ray
SLAUGHTER GANG I II III
RUTHLESS HEART I II III
By Willie Slaughter
FUK SHYT
By Blakk Diamond
DON'T F#CK WITH MY HEART I II
By Linnea
ADDICTED TO THE DRAMA I II III
IN THE ARM OF HIS BOSS II
By Jamila
YAYO I II III IV
A SHOOTER'S AMBITION I II
BRED IN THE GAME
By S. Allen
TRAP GOD I II III

RICH $AVAGE I II III

MONEY IN THE GRAVE I II III

By Martell Troublesome Bolden

FOREVER GANGSTA I II

GLOCKS ON SATIN SHEETS I II

By Adrian Dulan

TOE TAGZ I II III IV

LEVELS TO THIS SHYT I II

IT'S JUST ME AND YOU

By Ah'Million

KINGPIN DREAMS I II III

RAN OFF ON DA PLUG

By Paper Boi Rari

CONFESSIONS OF A GANGSTA I II III IV

CONFESSIONS OF A JACKBOY I II

By Nicholas Lock

I'M NOTHING WITHOUT HIS LOVE

SINS OF A THUG

TO THE THUG I LOVED BEFORE

A GANGSTA SAVED XMAS

IN A HUSTLER I TRUST

By Monet Dragun

CAUGHT UP IN THE LIFE I II III

THE STREETS NEVER LET GO I II

By Robert Baptiste

NEW TO THE GAME I II III

MONEY, MURDER & MEMORIES I II III

By **Malik D. Rice**

LIFE OF A SAVAGE I II III IV

A GANGSTA'S QUR'AN I II III IV

MURDA SEASON I II III
GANGLAND CARTEL I II III
CHI'RAQ GANGSTAS I II III IV
KILLERS ON ELM STREET I II III
JACK BOYZ N DA BRONX I II III
A DOPEBOY'S DREAM I II III
JACK BOYS VS DOPE BOYS I II III
COKE GIRLZ
COKE BOYS
By Romell Tukes
LOYALTY AIN'T PROMISED I II
By Keith Williams
QUIET MONEY I II III
THUG LIFE I II III
EXTENDED CLIP I II
A GANGSTA'S PARADISE
By **Trai'Quan**
THE STREETS MADE ME I II III
By **Larry D. Wright**
THE ULTIMATE SACRIFICE I, II, III, IV, V, VI
KHADIFI
IF YOU CROSS ME ONCE
ANGEL I II III IV
IN THE BLINK OF AN EYE
By **Anthony Fields**
THE LIFE OF A HOOD STAR
By Ca$h & Rashia Wilson
THE STREETS WILL NEVER CLOSE I II III
By K'ajji
CREAM I II III

THE STREETS WILL TALK

By Yolanda Moore

NIGHTMARES OF A HUSTLA I II III

By King Dream

CONCRETE KILLA I II III

VICIOUS LOYALTY I II

By Kingpen

HARD AND RUTHLESS I II

MOB TOWN 251

THE BILLIONAIRE BENTLEYS I II III

By Von Diesel

GHOST MOB

Stilloan Robinson

MOB TIES I II III IV V VI

SOUL OF A HUSTLER, HEART OF A KILLER

GORILLAZ IN THE TRENCHES

By SayNoMore

BODYMORE MURDERLAND I II III

THE BIRTH OF A GANGSTER I II

By Delmont Player

FOR THE LOVE OF A BOSS

By C. D. Blue

MOBBED UP I II III IV

THE BRICK MAN I II III IV

THE COCAINE PRINCESS I II III IV V

By King Rio

KILLA KOUNTY I II III IV

By Khufu

MONEY GAME I II

By Smoove Dolla

A GANGSTA'S KARMA I II

By FLAME

KING OF THE TRENCHES I II III

by **GHOST & TRANAY ADAMS**

QUEEN OF THE ZOO I II

By **Black Migo**

GRIMEY WAYS I II

By Ray Vinci

XMAS WITH AN ATL SHOOTER

By Ca$h & Destiny Skai

KING KILLA

By Vincent "Vitto" Holloway

BETRAYAL OF A THUG I II

By Fre$h

THE MURDER QUEENS I II

By Michael Gallon

TREAL LOVE

By Le'Monica Jackson

FOR THE LOVE OF BLOOD I II

By Jamel Mitchell

HOOD CONSIGLIERE I II

By Keese

PROTÉGÉ OF A LEGEND

By Corey Robinson

BORN IN THE GRAVE

By Self Made Tay

MOAN IN MY MOUTH

By XTASY

TORN BETWEEN A GANGSTER AND A GENTLEMAN

By J-BLUNT & Miss Kim

<u>BOOKS BY LDP'S CEO, CA$H</u>

TRUST IN NO MAN

TRUST IN NO MAN 2

TRUST IN NO MAN 3

BONDED BY BLOOD

SHORTY GOT A THUG

THUGS CRY

THUGS CRY 2

THUGS CRY 3

TRUST NO BITCH

TRUST NO BITCH 2

TRUST NO BITCH 3

TIL MY CASKET DROPS

RESTRAINING ORDER

RESTRAINING ORDER 2

IN LOVE WITH A CONVICT

LIFE OF A HOOD STAR

XMAS WITH AN ATL SHOOTER

Rich $avage 3

9 781958 111628